Igloo among Palms

The

Iowa

Short

Fiction

Award

University of

Iowa Press

Iowa City

Rod
Val
Moore

Igloo

among

Palms

The publication of this book is supported by a grant from the National Endowment for the Arts in Washington, D.C., a federal agency.

University of Iowa Press, Iowa City 52242

Copyright © 1994 by Rod Val Moore

Library of Congress Cataloging-in-Publication Data

Moore, Rod, 1952–

Igloo among palms / Rod Val Moore.

p.   cm.—(The Iowa short fiction award)

ISBN 0-87745-475-2

1. City and town life—California—Fiction.   2. City and town life—Mexico—Fiction.   3. Mexican-American Border Region—Fiction.   I. Title.   II. Series.

PS3563.O645I37   1994

813'.54—dc20   94-22499

CIP

01 00 99 98 97 96 95 94 C 5 4 3 2 1

For Lisa

Contents

ACKNOWLEDGMENTS

Stories in this collection appeared, in slightly
different form, in the following publications:
"Grimshaw's Mexico" in *Prairie Schooner*
and "Igloo among Palms" in the *Western
Humanities Review*.
For their encouragement and assistance, I am
especially grateful to Kate Haake, Bill
Wallis, Margaret Freeman, and the National
Endowment for the Arts.

Igloo among Palms

Grimshaw's Mexico

There are three stories in Sergeant Grimshaw's life which, if I string them together, may approximate a single story. The first one begins with an overworked Grimshaw being ordered by his precinct captain to take the next day off, to relax and go to the beach or the circus or the mountains. Grimshaw gladly accepted. And because Mrs. Grimshaw—her first name was Audrey—was sick with her summer allergies and had been pestering her husband to drive her to a certain obscure, vaguely illegal medical clinic in Baja, he chose to use his day off to finally get her down there and get her the medicine she claimed to need.

Years later, Grimshaw could recall just how Audrey had looked that day: simultaneously dark and glittering, dressed in black and gray tweed, eyes sparkling with what looked like allergy but really was a film of tears. Her loose charcoal suit was out of fashion even then, in 1952, and the bone-colored snood restraining her mass of hair and the tears in the mascara made her look like a war bride who had never been told about V-J Day.

For six-year-old Timothy the trip to Mexico was going to be the first time ever out of California and so a day for growing up a little. But the morning began with tantrums and reversions. Grimshaw had recently enrolled his son in the church-sponsored scouting program and now tyrannical Timothy insisted every morning, writhing and dancing away from his mother's touch, that he would wear nothing but his new, blueberry scout shirt with its epaulets and brass pins and official mustard yellow neckerchief. Audrey demanded, then implored Timothy to wear something else during the long, hot automobile trip.

"You do that to copy your father," she smirked at last, giving up the fight. "Cops, boy scouts, blue uniforms. But you are not a god-damned policeman; you are a little boy."

Grimshaw could not deny that he liked uniforms, nor that he had enlisted Timothy in the scouts mostly for the pleasure that came of displaying his boy to the world in a glow of semimartial golds and dress-code blues. Proper police blouse and trousers, in fact, were what the sergeant had already chosen for himself that morning. He knew he wouldn't be allowed to bring his gun across the border, but he buckled on an empty holster anyway, believing that in a foreign na-tion he should look as much like a cop, and as much like a designated guardian of American women and children, as possible.

Just before getting in the car Grimshaw took his son aside and helped him with the final details of his neckerchief, making sure that Tim had followed the scout rules of tucking his shirt collar under and tying the hanging tips of the scarf with a square knot. Then he pulled off Timothy's wolf cub neckerchief ring and in its place slipped a tin ring, one that he had dug out on a sudden inspiration from the bottom of his cuff-link box. Because the ring was engraved with a circular parade of tiny hula dancers and jaunty palm trees, Grimshaw told his son that it was made out of silver from the silver mines of Hawaii, but in fact he had won it long before in an arcade, dredging it up from a pile of other gewgaws with a little crane.

"It looks nice on the neckerchief," whispered Grimshaw, glancing sidelong at his exasperated wife. "Let's think of it as your first merit badge—awarded for bravery under fire."

Their destination that day was Puerto Niño, undeveloped and unromantic, hot and windy in a valley below sea level. The town was too far inland from the gulf to get much cool air and could boast of no attraction besides a number of factories, a church built of corrugated tin, and the notorious Clínica Goodman, which attracted a steady stream of Californians anxious to stock up on a new allergy medicine made from animal placentas. At two in the afternoon, after five hours of driving, they pulled into town. Audrey's first reaction—it was the first time she had spoken during the whole trip—was that she wasn't expecting so many factories and smokestacks, so many deserted streets.

"You wouldn't think," she said, "that they would need so many factories just to make tacos."

But this uncharitable and perhaps bigoted remark went unheard by Grimshaw, who was utterly lost and desperate to find his way without asking for help in a language he could not speak. He didn't hear a word Audrey said. Frowning and gripping the steering wheel as if it were somehow propping him up, he turned down one dirt road after another, each more unlikely looking than the last, until at length he pulled over in despair—and found that he had accidentally parked in front of the clinic. Audrey sullenly slipped out of the car, peered sharply back at Timothy for a moment, then disappeared inside.

"Well, what do you say we drive around some more," proposed Grimshaw in a jaunty tone of voice, "and really get to know the place." But Timothy was already halfway out of the car and it turned out that Grimshaw could do no more than follow his son across the street to an empty lot, where some boys about Timothy's age were playing baseball.

When Timothy paused on the edge of the lot and Grimshaw caught up with him, he put his hand on his son's shoulder and said something about the flatness of the country, the fact of being below sea level. He suddenly wanted Timothy to get an education. Two local women were walking toward them, and Grimshaw turned his son so he could see how they wore their hair in buns and dressed in several layers of old-fashioned calico aprons.

"Aren't they something?" he whispered to Timothy. But all the time he was thinking that the women looked wrong, not strange enough. Why had he imagined that they would be wearing nothing but black and walking in circles around a vast chalk-white plaza? Puerto Niño, it seemed, didn't have a plaza, and there was nothing white anywhere—just yellow dirt streets, the chalky blue of the below-sea-level sky, and the black walls of a factory that reared just behind the baseball diamond like a mesa made of dull desert coal.

The two ladies came closer, and it turned out they were candy vendors, with baskets full of both brilliant cellophane-wrapped nuggets and stranger, somewhat frightening items rolled by hand in unlabeled scraps of brown paper. Grimshaw, peering into the two baskets, heard the vendors talking. But it was to each other, not to him.

"I wonder," he said, "why they walk together when they must be competing for the same customers?" Then he stole a glance at the ladies to see if they might have understood him and thought him rude. But their faces remained composed and sad, and they kept talking to each other in a language that Grimshaw was pretty sure could not be Spanish.

"Listen," he whispered again to Timothy. "Listen to them talk. That's the Indian language."

Finally, by means of hand signals, Grimshaw picked out and paid for a fat round jawbreaker that came packaged in reassuringly glossy paper, which he then unwrapped and placed on Timothy's waiting tongue with the seriousness of a priest offering a wafer. Meanwhile a local boy had wandered over from the diamond and seemed to be gesturing to Timothy to come over and play baseball. Timothy looked up at his father and Grimshaw realized that what the boy wanted was permission to go play. He looked like a baseball star already, Grimshaw thought, with his cheek puffed out with candy instead of tobacco. Then, like a clean-up batter, Timothy solemnly spit out the jawbreaker, grimaced, and ran off with his new friend, clutching at the tails of his neckerchief to keep them from bouncing against his face.

Grimshaw found a bench nearby that seemed meant for spectators, and he sat down to watch; but then, although the wood was cold and comfortable in the heat, he stood up again. Discovering his son's spit-out candy near his shoe, he ground it down into the dirt, out of sight, burying it in this way out of a fear that because they were in what he thought of as the Third World some child would come along and pop the dirty candy in his mouth.

Meanwhile, the baseball game had resumed, with Timothy, Grimshaw noted with a strange pride, at second base. All the bases were marked by tires that had been painted a dazzling white. The pitcher for Timothy's team was an extremely thin and comically flexible boy, a skeleton boy, no more than eight years old, who could throw the ball and get it over the plate pretty well, but who dove straight to the ground after each pitch, as if afraid of the ball coming right back at him from the batter. This never happened. It was true that most of the kids played a little rough. Sometimes a few of them, Timothy included, would go into fits, screaming and rolling on the ground, giving up their field positions to grab each other and wrestle, rub faces triumphantly in the dirt, tear their torn shirts a little more.

As the hour grew long Grimshaw ended up sitting down and finally stretching out fully on the wooden bench, reflecting how Audrey, when she came out of the clinic, was going to have a fit to see Timothy so filthy, so renegade, with his shirt hanging in tatters from his shoulders, his scout neckerchief tied around his forehead pirate style, his knuckles badly cut, as was to be discovered later, from a rock-hard fast ball that had smashed his poor fingers against the bat.

But Audrey didn't come out of the clinic and the game, such as it was, went on. Another hour dragged by. Sergeant Grimshaw half dozed, lifting one hand luxuriously to do nothing more than stir into a kind of whirlpool a cloud of afternoon insects that hovered just above his face. Later he thought he had discovered that over-the-border clouds were fundamentally different from California clouds—more yellow than white, more dirty—but soon he resolved that those were just the clouds of that particular day in Puerto Niño, the clouds above a place that was warm and windy and below sea level, a town that somehow seemed to draw the clouds down to it and stain them with its industrial yellows and browns.

Finally Grimshaw slept.

And awoke, and shot straight up at the sound, like a gunshot, of his wife's voice. It was dark, and Audrey, unable to see either of them, was calling out their names in a fearful yet piercing warble. Grimshaw arose guiltily from his bench, instinctively brushing imaginary dirt from his trousers, and stumbled forward to meet her in the blue gloom, his eyes finding her by focusing on the white paper bag she held in her hands.

"What's in the bag, hon?" he called out sweetly, stupidly. He could see now that she held onto it with a strange determination, like a balloon that would float away if she didn't hold tight or would burst if she squeezed too hard. Timothy appeared then too. He came up to where his parents stood, two of his newfound friends in comical tow, and this performing trio staggered in a circle around the Grimshaws, giggling and whispering, their arms locked around each other's shoulders. One of them was the skinny pitcher, who now appeared, Grimshaw noted with surprise, to be much older than the others, almost high school age. The three of them were dirty as pirates, but Timothy was the blackest and the scruffiest of all, with a cake of blood below his nose that looked like a Hitler mustache. But what amazed Grimshaw, and kept him from getting mad, was the Spanish. Timothy had learned Spanish. And now he laughed and—or at least so it seemed to Grimshaw—chattered in the new language, as if he had been studying and practicing for days instead of hours.

Then, what Grimshaw had suddenly hoped wouldn't happen, happened. Timothy turned to them, to his parents, and jabbered at them to their faces, either entirely forgetting his English or realizing that they couldn't understand him and so just wanting to kid them, to show off for them.

"Buenas tardes," he sang out, while his dark-haired friends stepped back and stared, suddenly serious and timid with enormous, gleaming black eyes. "Somos los campeones de baseball."

When Grimshaw heard these impossible words springing from the sweet, blood-stained mouth of his son, he felt an irresistible pity, not for Timothy but for Audrey, who just then moved closer to him, as if in fear. Instead of yelling or crying, as he half expected, she just clutched her white paper bag closer to her stomach with one hand and took hold of Grimshaw's arm with the other. He guessed what she was thinking: that the dirt and the blood and the Spanish were her own fault, because she had made them come to this place.

Yet Grimshaw, as soon as he sensed Audrey's discomfort, gently pulled his arm from her grasp and was surprised to discover in himself two emotions, both quite different and strangely superior, he thought, to hers. One was delight in Timothy's comically easy entry into another world; the other was disappointment that he himself had wasted his one afternoon in Baja just lying there, that he hadn't even really looked around Puerto Niño, or gotten involved—that now they would have to climb in the car and drive all night back to the house, just when he was ready, exhausted as he was, to grab hold of the situation, to really look at things, to really get to know the place.

The second story is from years later, when Timothy was grown and had entered his senior year in high school. The Grimshaws had known for a long time that their son, in spite of pretty low grades in everything, was relatively enthusiastic about biology, and they paid careful attention whenever he talked in his perfunctory way about wanting to get into medical school. One day, in fact, Grimshaw was surprised to hear Timothy announce that he wanted someday to get a job as a coroner, but he kept his distaste for coroners and their work to himself and mumbled a few words of encouragement.

It was around the same time that Timothy declared his intention to enter the school science fair. He didn't know what he wanted to do for it, just that it ought to have something to do with biology. The announcement came as a surprise, because the boy's extracurricular activities had been limited to a few afternoons of B-Team football, despite the Grimshaws' efforts to get him to join an activities club or run for student office. The science fair, Grimshaw told his wife, was the first sign they'd had that Timothy was starting to wake up to the idea of responsibility and self-motivation.

But several weeks went by, and there was no indication that Timothy had set to work on any kind of science project. Finally Grimshaw thought he should say something.

"If there's going to be a project," Grimshaw frowned, sitting on the edge of Timothy's bed while the boy lay back on a pillow and drank a can of soda, "then maybe you should let me help out, get something going in the workshop."

Timothy's eyes widened. He put down the can of soda and seemed genuinely concerned; but he had no answer, because in fact there hadn't been any progress in his thinking at all, and he couldn't come up with an idea then and there beyond wanting to do "something about the human body."

As the day of the science fair drew closer, Grimshaw felt more and more sorry for the boy and racked his brains every day for an idea, even going so far as to talk to the county coroner, an unfriendly man whom Grimshaw sometimes had to meet on business, though always with great reluctance. But the coroner was warmly, unexpectedly interested in Timothy's "case," and when Grimshaw arrived home that night he bore a list, scribbled down by the coroner on a coffee shop napkin, of fascinating and challenging ideas for projects. At the dinner table, after Grimshaw had solemnly unfolded the napkin, with its ballpoint jottings and tears, like a scientist unrolling the plans for a space rocket, Timothy impatiently announced that it was too late, that he now had his own idea. Ignoring the pained, deliberate fastidiousness with which his father slowly crumpled and pushed aside the precious list, Timothy hurried on to explain how his project would work. By building a special kind of instructional display called a "Teaching Skeleton," he said, he was going to teach visitors to the science fair to identify and memorize something he had always had trouble memorizing, that is, the names of the bones in the body. The main thing was to somehow put together a life-size skeletal model. They would have to do a fair amount of electrical wiring too. And it would all have to come together within five days.

At first the proposal did not go over well. Timothy and his father argued for a while, though really they didn't have much reason to. Grimshaw built up his anger about the wasted meeting with the coroner into something more than it was; in fact, one of the ideas written on the discarded napkin was almost identical to his son's. Finally Grimshaw shrugged, laughed, and promised Timothy he would do everything he could to help build the Teaching Skeleton.

"The main thing is to make this a family project," Grimshaw proclaimed, sawing at his steak with exaggerated pleasure. "Timothy, you've got the good idea, I can help with the cutting and wiring, and maybe your mom could help us out by looking up a skeleton chart or a poster or something."

But Audrey, quietly pushing her own food around the plate during the whole discussion, was visibly disturbed. Finally she put down her fork, stared at her steak, and then, with a sniff of amusement, perhaps of sarcasm, left the room.

Undaunted, Timothy and his father spent the next five evenings in the garage, snipping out larger-than-life-size human bone shapes from sheet metal, then hinging them together with neat little rivets, coating everything with ivory house paint and drilling holes in such a way that each bone, just as envisioned from the beginning by Timothy, would have its own red light bulb, cranberry size, wired into the center of its flat surface. Neither of them was good with a pen, so the aspects of the skull that had to be drawn in, like the eye sockets, the jagged cranial fissures, and the grinning molars, were not, as Grimshaw remarked, going to win them any points for artistry.

Grimshaw strung up the light bulbs in the bones in such a way that the wires leading from the lights to the identification panel—a wooden plaque with rows of buttons and labels spelling out words like "ulna" and "radius"—were almost invisible. The wires were made long enough so that the panel didn't have to sit on the floor but could be placed on a table a few feet in front of the Teaching Skeleton. The idea was that visitors to Timothy's installation would consult the panel, find the name of some bone they wished to identify, and press the appropriate button. The participants could that way continue through all the buttons until in fact they had more or less mastered the names of the majority of important human bones.

One funny argument came up as they worked together. Timothy had suddenly decided, the night before the fair, that there had to be two identification panels, one with the names of the bones in English and one in Spanish. Grimshaw was surprised by the idea, and recalled for the first time in years the long-ago baseball game in Baja, and the miraculous Spanish his son had cheerfully and innocently rattled off in what seemed in perspective like a rare moment of brilliance. Now he noticed with something like satisfaction that his son could no more speak a word of Spanish than he could, and had to look up the names of all the bones in a dictionary, along with the very word "bone" itself. At any rate, Grimshaw tried to convince his son that the second language would be a distraction, and that the work of building another panel would mean that they might not finish in time. But Grimshaw, working late at night, after Timothy had gone to bed, went ahead and started to build a second panel and had even cut a couple of pieces of wood before he realized he was being idiotic, and that the second language could of course be written onto the original panel, that there was room for each Spanish label to go directly under each English label. Using the list of translations that Timothy had copied out, it took him only an hour to cautiously squeeze out the Spanish on a pistol-shaped label maker.

The next morning they got to school early and were let into the gymnasium, with the other competitors, to set things up. Timothy and his dad suspended the metal skeleton on wires that they attached to the rim of a basketball hoop and plugged everything into an outlet that a janitor revealed by unscrewing a brass cap in the middle of the floor. When the doors were finally opened for the waiting crowd, Grimshaw took up a spot some distance away, where he could watch people's reactions but not make Timothy nervous, and he noticed after awhile that, besides the judges, who spent a long time pushing buttons and whispering, not many people stopped to talk to Timothy and try out the lights. Grimshaw started to feel uncomfortable. He realized from some comments that he overheard, and from his own observations, that Timothy's project was not nearly as entertaining or as technically sophisticated as some others. The roughly drawn, delicately suspended skeleton with its occasional jewelry of ruby lights began to look more and more to him like some kind of flimsy, comical decoration for a Halloween party, something that would be thrown away with the rotten jack-o'-lanterns. When Audrey appeared and paused to peer down at the rows of buttons, Grimshaw was certain she would find it all contemptible, and he walked away a few steps to avoid her seeing him.

Finally, at the end of the viewing hour, after all the projects had been examined by the judges, Timothy and Audrey and Grimshaw, along with all the other parents and children, sat together in the auditorium to hear the judges' decisions. As names were read out, winners sprang forward to accept their trophies. First prize went for a system of filters which slowly converted a cup of sea water to three-fourths of a cup of drinking water. Second prize was for a power lawn mower that had somehow been converted—Grimshaw couldn't imagine how this would work but applauded furiously anyway—to use its own grass cuttings as its fuel.

Then came the startler. "Third prize," droned the principal, squinting at a three-by-five card, "goes to Timothy Grimshaw, for his instructional skeleton, which, as the judges indicate, has the added virtue of bilingual instructions, and so makes its knowledge available to a wider spectrum of viewers."

The principal looked up, frowning, waiting for Timothy Grimshaw to step forward and receive his little wood and chrome trophy. But at the moment that the principal had announced his name, perhaps even a second before, Audrey had grabbed hold of Timothy's arm and painfully pulled him toward her to keep him from standing. The two of them sat that way for a long time, the boy unable to move without a struggle, unwilling to look his mother in the face. Finally Grimshaw, sitting on the other side of his son, looked over to see what was wrong.

It was only then that Audrey spoke. Then it became obvious that she had been waiting a very long time to say something, and she shoved Timothy back a little to lean forward and point her face, like a finger, at her husband.

"Why don't you go up for the prize," she whispered, almost whistling the words. "After all, aren't you the one who did the work? Aren't you the pathetic genius who beat out all these children?"

Then she was done. She had said what she wanted to say. She let go of Timothy, and he stumbled forward, rubbing his arm, to accept his trophy.

"Thank you very much," he grinned into the microphone, holding his trophy near his ear as if he were about to forward pass it into the crowd. "Thank you very much and muchas gracias."

The third story takes us back to Baja, to a time shortly after Timothy had graduated from college and finally found his dream job, working as a coroner's assistant in another state, and he and his new wife, a park ranger, had moved halfway across the continent. That left Audrey and Grimshaw alone; but soon, despite Audrey's claims that her allergies and other ills were worsening and that she needed Grimshaw's allegiance and assistance more than ever, they separated—only to get back together after a short period of time. During the several months of their separation, Grimshaw, seeking at one stroke to change his life in all its particulars, retired from the force and prepared himself for a life of travel. When he moved back in with Audrey it was only on the condition that she agree to his travel plans and go wherever he said they ought to go without complaining or asking to go back home.

So it was that the Grimshaws found themselves in Baja, talking somewhat too solemnly about how the trip represented a chance to "get to know each other again." But things did not go smoothly. For one thing, Grimshaw got the idea, once they were down there, that the two of them ought to scout around for a little hacienda they could buy, a place where they could live comfortably on his pension and that they could use as a base for further adventures here and there. Nothing ever came of the idea—the only places that the real estate agents were willing to show them were American-style vacation condominiums, and Grimshaw, to Audrey's poorly concealed disgust, kept talking about "going native" and was always trying to talk her into the idea of buying one of the many run-down but vaguely picturesque adobes they passed on their way from resort condo to resort condo.

One day the two of them were sitting in an outdoor cafe under some arches, drinking fresh fruit juice after fresh fruit juice, Audrey going along with an idea her husband was talking up at the time about a diet based on natural foods and moderate fasting. The city they had ended up in was much farther south than Puerto Niño and to Grimshaw felt a little closer to his old idea of chalky hills and women in black. At the same time, contrary to his dream, the sky was not at all clear, despite the high altitude, but soggy and overcast. In fact, the low gray mist seemed less like weather than some kind of industrial effluent. Cars that came around the nearest corner—cars sometimes driven, Grimshaw observed with a twinge of bitter amusement, by old women in black—would occasionally squeal their tires just a few feet from the Americans' sidewalk table, at the same time spewing out a rancid diesel exhaust, a smoke that slightly intoxicated Grimshaw. But just across the street was a dark green park with a little bandstand, a baroque and bright red cupola that cheered Grimshaw considerably and made him forget about the unbearable air, about the pointless and cheerless vacation.

While they sat silently nursing their juices, a variety of itinerant vendors made their way among the tables, coming up to customers with their characteristically careless and pessimistic come-ons. Of course there was the legion of shoe-shine boys but also any number of middle-aged and older men selling strange dime-store wares: dish soap, little cars and bicycles made out of wire, pairs of old-fashioned heavy steel scissors. Then there were the entertainers: one particularly polite man wanted to sketch their pictures, and they both sat quietly for what struck both of them, when he was done, as amazingly accurate portraits. Someone else wanted to serenade all the restaurant patrons on a homemade violin, but they gestured him away after getting a dose of woebegone screeching.

"That was something that sounded," Audrey joked after thinking for a minute, "not like Montezuma's quickstep, but more like Montezuma's funeral march."

Then Grimshaw pointed out an approaching itinerant who was considerably more mysterious than the others. This one was stripped to the waist and wore tight red pants, leather gloves, and a tight leather cowl with large eye holes, the kind that some theatrical wrestlers wear. But the fellow was old, as was clear from the posture and the twirl of white hairs against the coppery breasts, and he wandered about the tables in an old man's precise and deadpan fashion, lugging a heavy wooden box the size of a small suitcase. He would present himself at each table with a dignified bow that clashed with the outrageous costume, and when the patrons refused him, he showed none of the desperation or rudeness of some of the other itinerants. Yet whatever it was he had to offer, table after table turned him down. Eventually the half-naked old man ended up at the table next to the Grimshaws, where a noisy knot of American college boys, evidently all a little drunk, applauded his introduction and could hardly wait to slap their dollars down on the wet table.

The box he carried, Grimshaw could see now, was a neatly homemade affair of plywood and silvery screws and had been labeled, in black stencil letters, with the words "Batery-Man/Artista de Voltaje." Below the lettering there was a single enormous dial, numbered from one to ten, and on the other side, attached by bare copper wires, hung a pair of short steel rods, or batons, as burnished as old silver candlesticks. It was easy to see from the gestures and expressions that the old man had bet the students that they would not be able to hold the rods bare-handed and withstand the sting of the electricity while the voltage was slowly boosted with the rotation of the thick black dial.

To prove that such electrical punishment was possible, to show that a given number of volts could be endured by a human being, the battery man began with an auto-electrocution. Spreading his legs and striking a rigid posture, he theatrically peeled off his gloves, snatched up the cylinders, and held his arms out wide, like a supplicant, indicating to one of the college boys, with a solemn bow of his head, to begin to rotate the dial. By this time a number of people had twisted their chairs around and were craning their necks to watch the unusual performance. As the dial reached the number three, the voltage artist closed his eyes serenely, and at around five, squinted them tightly shut. But it was not until the student had turned the pointer up to somewhere between six and seven that the old man signaled to him to slack off, to turn the dial back. After gingerly setting down the cylinders on top of the battery, the voltage artist gave a sign that six was the significant number. If anyone could get past that point on the dial, they would win the pile of bills on the table.

Then it was the first customer's turn. To the accompaniment of laughter and exaggerated bravado, one of the students took up the batons, stood up in the same stiffened posture, and indicated that he was ready to go. The voltage artist, nodding deferentially, turned the dial. The first mark, and the second, were reached with no obvious effects except the student's nervous smile. But by three the smile was gone, his comrades were completely silent, and the boy was obviously experiencing some discomfort, if not pain. On four he suddenly let go, letting the batons fall to the table, shaking his head violently, shouting angrily at a friend who tried to get him to take a drink. Grimshaw suspected that at that point none of the other students would try it, but one after another they did, with the result that none of them even got as far around the dial as the first one. What surprised Grimshaw were the ones who tried it more than once, slapping another dollar on the table each time, as if they couldn't quite believe that the old man could outperform them, as if they didn't understand that people can learn, through practice and imperceptible increase, to stand anything, and can in effect train themselves to turn up all kinds of real and figurative dials.

When at last it seemed that no one had the nerve to take another dose of electrical grief, the old man calmly peeled the leather mask off his head—revealing a shock of white hair and the face of a pure-blooded Indian—and stuffed the pile of dollars inside. Then, as if on impulse, as if suddenly changing his mind, the voltage artist picked up the two steel rods, repositioned himself and, still smiling, still nodding, had one of the students turn up the dial one more time. By the time he was back up to six, quite a crowd had gathered, and even the losers were applauding him on to more. Except perhaps for the occasional trembling in the jowls, the old man was composed in his features, and cast his ice-cold eyes—the eyes, thought Grimshaw, of a great chief, of a Geronimo—around the faces of the crowd, all the while nodding at intervals for the dial to go up another notch, and then another. Now everyone was deathly quiet. Finally, the dial was up to ten, and most of the crowd had backed away, as if expecting an explosion. To taunt them, the old man held out the rods and laughed, daring anyone to grab hold of them with him and share the jolt.

That was when Grimshaw wondered if he couldn't do it too.

While watching the gringo students take their shocks, sipping occasionally at his juice, and glancing at his wife, who had long ago grown bored with the performance and was hardly paying attention anymore, Grimshaw had begun to wonder if he wasn't making a mistake, if he wasn't getting ready to leave Baja, like the last time, without doing something foreign and unforgettable, without seizing some previously unimaginable, or if imaginable then terrifying, opportunity.

"Audrey," he muttered, "do you think I should try it?"

But she wasn't listening or didn't understand.

"No," she said. "No more. I really haven't liked any of these juices. Do you think they would serve me a soft drink?"

Somehow her response became Grimshaw's signal to lunge. Before Audrey, who suddenly saw his intention and started shouting out something, could stop him, Grimshaw had leapt out of his chair and, without grabbing them away from the Indian, taken hold of the extended ends of the batons, thinking to at least share with the old man some part of that horrible current. Here at last, he thought, squeezing the metal, here was the chance to do as Timothy had done, to play some Mexican baseball, to learn to speak Spanish in a moment, and he waited for the furious shock that would stand his hair on end, turn his body transparent, as in a cartoon, to show the glowing, aching skeleton underneath.

But there was nothing, no shock at all, and though at first he wondered if there were not enough current for two men, he soon understood that it was a trick, that there was no current, that the old man had some secret way of turning it on and off whenever he wanted. That left Grimshaw and the Indian just standing there face to face, holding onto the rods, their fingers overlapping a little on the dead metal, their eyes uncomfortably locked, both of them wondering what the other one would do next. Then Grimshaw, becoming aware of Audrey standing frozen in horror just behind him, and aware also of the fascinated crowd staring at him from all sides, trembled a little for everyone's benefit, hoping to make them think, to make himself think, that he was taking all that juice, that the two of them, the two old men, were the world champions of electricity, that they could survive everything that the battery could dish out, and more.

Igloo
among
Palms

If for no other reason than to get out of the house, Tod said yes he would do it, he would volunteer for the emergency dry ice delivery job.

"Are you sure, Toddy?" asked Ike, his big brother, owner of the ice business. He looked up from where he was crawling on hands and knees with a smelly can of malt liquor in one hand and a bug-spray aerosol in the other, showering poison on a poor red and black beetle as it battled its way ever more slowly across the linoleum. At that point it was already one in the morning.

"I'm sure," groaned Tod. He was a tall boy and stood up slowly, painfully, like a stork that unfolds itself to fly.

Then Ike went through the details of the job: that it was only the

Junior Boy Supermarket in Rosetta and that they needed a delivery PDQ because one of the long freezers had gone down, and Juventino the regular driver wouldn't work at night, and if they didn't get the dry ice in there before long, Junior Boy was going to lose an inventory of frozen confections to the tune of two thousand dollars or thereabouts.

Not that the dry ice would keep Tod cool as he drove through the night heat. The only way it would air-condition the car, Ike told him, was if you kept the windows rolled up, and, if you kept the windows rolled up, you'd die of carbon dioxide poisoning.

"Because that's all dry ice is," he went on, though Tod already knew the facts and understood perfectly, from living with Ike, how dry ice is nothing more than carbon dioxide gas that's been squeezed into a chamber so pressurized that it solidifies into white smoky blocks that burn your fingers, if you touch them, just as badly as would red-hot burners on a stove.

"But why don't I just take the truck," Tod asked, "and put the dry ice in the back, in the bed of the truck?"

"Because you can't," said his brother, who tried every day, usually without success, to get Tod to help out with the business. "Truck's broke down. That leaves the Carluxe, Toddy. But Junior Boy only needs six hundred pounds, and we'll be able to get some of that in the trunk and the rest in the back seat."

The Carluxe was an old vermilion-colored Imperial, fantastically large, that had been in the family for years. It was Tod, as a verbally precocious child, who had named it first the Car Deluxe and later simply the Carluxe.

The brothers moved swiftly after the details had been worked out and they had the car loaded and ready to drive in a few minutes. Then Tod took hold of the wheel, inched backward down the driveway, hit the gas, and soon was unchained and over the speed limit, finally and maybe forever on his own. It felt good to be going, not because of the favor he was doing his brother, but because of the feeling of going and going. Going to be getting gone. Yet by the time he could really open it up on the late-night highway, he was disappointed to find that out there the heat in the fields was as unbearable as the air-conditioned cold at Ike's house, and that the smell of dark green crops and their dust of malathion was as smothering as Ike's sour malt liquor. There was no moon out, and between Giza Beach and Rosetta there were no landmarks, no streetlights or billboards, just the narrow asphalt that extended like a dreary dark canal between acres of carrots on the left and strips of dark alfalfa on the right.

"Not the scenic route," Tod shouted over the radio, already as bored as he always knew he would be in the ice business. But the boredom for some reason sparked him and strengthened his determination to try to please his older brother for once, try to make this an outstanding delivery, the greatest delivery in the history of dry ice. Not as proof, of course, of wanting to get in on the business, but more as a silent apology for never having any intention to.

Immediately Tod relaxed, and then felt sleepy. To stay awake he drove with one hand down, on the bottom of the chrome and bakelite steering wheel, and one hand up, poised near his cheek, to sometimes slap himself rhythmically and lightly in time to the tinny rock and roll, in this way keeping himself half-awake enough to wonder if maybe when he got back from the delivery he could get up the nerve to tell Ike he was moving out. Occasionally he would glance in the rearview mirror at the six carefully arranged blocks of dry ice, all tightly wrapped in thick brown butcher paper and bound with scratchy twine, all still giving off their thin and slightly poisonous fog, like old cardboard suitcases leaking ghosts.

He thought, It is at least ninety holy degrees, and it's hours since the sun went down.

He thought, It's going to be hard to stay awake for half an hour, and I should try singing or reciting poetry or *something*. And he switched off the radio.

Try humming something when you're drowsy on the road, he recalled being told, and tried it, but his tuneless voice broke off by itself and he thought, I am like that red and black beetle on the linoleum and the dry ice is the bug spray Ike is using to get me.

Later there were thousands of dead leaves blowing across the road in front of him, round and noisy as rocks, sometimes spinning into whorls that lost themselves beneath his advancing headlights. The road was spookily empty for miles. Then, with the suddenness of a dream, a creature materialized out of the darkness. It was a lone hitchhiker, a man with eyes lit up like a startled deer, and he appeared at the far perimeter of Tod's headlights a hundred yards ahead, at the side of the highway, his legs whipped and circled by the stream of leaves.

Tod didn't know what to do. He couldn't say to himself, I should stop, or I'd better not stop. He checked his digital watch and saw that it was six minutes after two. Giza Beach was only five miles behind, and the car was already pushing through the heavy sea-level air at eighty miles per hour. Still lost in thought, Tod drove right past the gesturing figure at the side of the road. Then he did hit the brakes, but tentatively tapped the gas again, tapped the brakes, swallowed, then veered the Imperial rightward so that its tires crunched down onto the shoulder and the speedometer needle dropped to between five and ten miles per hour.

There was a strange thing with the hitchhiker. Somehow he must have run ahead—though how anyone could have moved so fast Tod could never understand—because suddenly there he was in the headlights again, windmilling his arms, and Tod had to swerve to avoid an accident and even then thought that at the last moment he must have clipped him because when the Imperial finally scraped to a complete stop and Tod took a look in the rearview mirror the man was getting up from the dirt and staring at his palms.

"I'm okay, I'm okay," he shouted.

It was a bespectacled and bearded man, and he stood for a moment at the back of the car, grinning, his glasses and his teeth now lit up bright red, like safety reflectors, from the brake lights.

Tod was amazed to find his heart beating fast. But then the hitchhiker jerked open the passenger door, flopped down beside Tod, leaned so close that their shoulders grazed, and tossed his daypack in back with the ice—and then it occurred to Tod that the guy was all right, that despite the long dirty hair and beard, the baseball cap, the eyeglasses secured in the back by an athlete's elastic, the hitchhiker's face somehow did not say I am that psychopath that has chosen to kill you, but said I am a harmless nobody, I am guileless and guiltless, I am more frightened of you right now than you probably are of me.

"You know what?" gasped the hitchhiker. "You didn't hit me. It was close, but no cigar. In fact, just the opposite. You rescued me. You know that you're a saint, don't you? A fucking *saint*. You know that? You are one holy fucking savior in one man's hour of need."

"Been waiting a long time then?" Tod asked, uncomfortable with the gratitude, frowning as he maneuvered the car smoothly out onto the highway and slowly regained speed.

"Not that long, my man. What I mean is, being picked up on a night like this—hot as the hobs of hell, as they say—by someone carrying a load of ice in a classy old red Imperial. Far fucking out."

This hitchhiker, thought Tod, is from somewhere not around here, but beyond that he couldn't place the gliding, somewhat over-salivated accent, or quite know what to make of the comment about the ice except to know for sure that the guy could not have known about the ice when he put his thumb out for a ride.

"We call it the Carluxe," smiled Tod, experiencing a peace that sometimes came over him when preparing to speak of things he knew to be indisputable and true. "And this kind of ice, dry ice, won't cool us off much. It's pure carbon dioxide. It's got to be enclosed to work, you see, to get things cold, and we've got to keep our windows down or we'll choke on the stuff. That's why I can't turn on the air conditioner."

"You know I only thumb rides at night, to stay out of the goddamn heat," continued the hitchhiker, showing no sign of having understood about the ice. "During the day I sleep. Somewhere in the shade if I can. You know, in somebody's barn or even out in the fields. Even then it's hard to sleep. Wish I had me an igloo made out of that dry ice, though, when I try to go to sleep tomorrow."

Tod let it go. It wasn't worth explaining twice. There was a silence while Tod sniffed at an herbal scent of Chapstick or throat lozenges that had come in the car with the hitchhiker.

"Originally, I am from Texas," announced the vagabond seriously, staring ahead at the highway and pronouncing the words very carefully, as if unveiling the week's winning lottery numbers. "And my name is Luther. Do you know that I've been doing this for years, living on a few dollars at a time? And I *mean* a few dollars too. Five here, ten there. Now I'm aiming myself at my girlfriend and I feel like—" And he sang the next part. "—a horny leettle monkey goin' back to its leetle monkey tree."

Then they rode for a mile, two miles.

"I know that feeling," said Tod, nodding in so approving a way that the lie felt very truthful, and very wise.

Two more miles.

"So," smiled Tod, trying to keep the talk alive, afraid to ask Luther what it was he meant when he said he'd been doing *this* for years. What was *this*? But then asking it.

"So what is it you do, Luther, while you're waiting for rides?"

That was Luther's button. That was exactly the question that Luther seemed to have been waiting for. He drew himself up like a Texas senator and then spoke, and recounted in some detail how he marched along the side of the road each night, listening to the insect music of the huge agribusiness landscape, taking a few vegetables from the fucked-up margins of the fields, turning to stick his thumb out whenever headlights came into view, using the silence between cars to ruminate at length on subjects such as the danger of malathion and other insecticides to farm workers, the decline of the small family farmer, the reports of guerrilla war in Mexico. Tod found out, then, that Luther was the kind of person, so unlike himself, who could talk and talk, who could spring from thought to thought, fact to fact—that Luther was the kind who would lean close to share little secrets, to talk on and on with a cold monotone persistence which sent strange shivers through Tod's knees and thighs and made him press harder and harder on the Imperial's accelerator pedal. The one thing that Tod kept thinking about was Luther's strange way of leaning close to whisper but not speaking in Tod's ear, instead just staring straight ahead at the highway, cramping one arm to run his fingers through his Chapstick-scented beard, finally taking off his complicated glasses and wearily covering his eyes with his hands but still talking and talking with his vaguely persuasive Texas accent and his way of stretching out his body on the seat straight as a board, even with his hand over his eyes, only to fumble idly with something, a set of keys perhaps, in his front blue jeans pocket.

The other thing that Tod kept thinking about was that talking to the hitchhiker was like conducting an interview but without having to ask questions. Luther provided the questions and then the answers. "Are the Mexicans going to start a war up here too, maybe in Sonora?" he asked. "No," he answered, "even though this is Zapata country, the agrarian reform is stronger here." And so on.

But Tod could not keep up with Luther's talk show. It had turned into something about aggression and cowardice and what Luther almost shouted about the "inevitability of one class dominating the other," and Tod suspended his attention after awhile in order to focus more sharply on himself and on the highway with its endless hyphenation and giant dreamy green exit signs on the periphery of everything. Sleepily, he decided he would like to tell the hitchhiker—if the hitchhiker were anyone but Luther—some story of his own. But there was no story to be told there and then. For the first time Tod wished he did work at his brother's ice plant, among the Mexicans, because there, he thought, there must be some of the storytelling and class struggle that seemed now to be missing from his life.

But then Tod's thoughts blurred, his eyelids grew heavy as nickels. He dozed off for a fraction of a second and his head fell through space for a moment, hurtled down toward his breast until a reflex, full of adrenaline and panic, snapped it back up straight.

"Did you know," he blurted, realizing that the hitchhiker had been silent a long time, staring out the window, and hadn't noticed his fleeting snooze, "that all these carrot fields out there used to be a dry lake bed? Do you know where the largest dry lake bed in the world is? Do you know where they get the gas to make dry ice?"

Then, when there was no reply, just Luther's herbal odor lingering for a moment in the air, Tod cleared some part of his mind and told what little more he knew about the ice plant. He explained to Luther about the enormous cold room, and about how the ice cubes and the ice blocks were manufactured, how they made the wet ice clear as diamonds, not milky or white like refrigerator ice. And he somewhat clumsily described how they concocted the dry ice—a wonderful substance that exists on the border between solid and gas—and how dry ice is used for more than just the spooky effect in punch bowls and rock concerts but also is important in a variety of industrial processes that in turn drive the national economy.

Then Tod's stream of unadorned truth broke off, and before he could go any further, before he could move forward to a story that he thought he could make up about the ice plant, he felt utterly empty, just plain out of mental fuel. He could see that Luther the vagabond had changed again—except that this time he was stretched out straight, his hand in his pocket, all in all looking much larger and stranger than when he had first clambered into the car. He had done something to his hair, taken off his baseball cap and used a girl's barrette to arrange it in a wild bun atop his head, and in the interior gloom of the Imperial he looked to Tod like some kind of monstrous bearded businesswoman.

"What did you say the name—" began Luther, finally moving and gesturing again, taking his hand out of his pants pocket to daub deftly at his lips with his balm. "What did you say the name of your ice company was?"

"I'm not sure I did say. But anyway it's not my ice company. I don't even work there. It's my brother's ice company and sometimes I do him some big favor. Tonight I'm delivering this dry ice to Rosetta. The Mexicans don't work at night. But the day of the explosion—the big explosion—I was just minding the office for a few minutes while everyone was out on delivery."

Tod felt a tiny choke in his throat, as if he were about to cry. The lie had been told, and was unforgivable. Now, what would be his punishment? But only a long silence followed. What explosion, Luther was supposed to say. What big explosion? But Luther was busy with the window on his side, trying to roll it down, discovering with a whistle that it was already down all the way, and then thrusting his head far out into the darkness, as if he were trying to get as far away as he could from the claustrophobia of the cab, or, Tod couldn't help thinking, from the claustrophobia of sin.

With a fluid twist of his whole body, Luther drew his head back in. His face was flushed with the late night heat, but it appeared to Tod that he had not gone back to his initial good humor or entertaining pedantry. In fact, it looked as if he had breathed in with the farm air a new and unexplainable power. His ponytail had come undone, his nostrils flared, and he sat erect in the cab, like a man wearing a spinal brace, his hair spitting out behind him in the breeze. Then Tod saw that his passenger was fiddling with something, tossing something from one hand to the other.

"Wow," said Tod, barely able to get the words out, but not afraid. "That's a knife."

It wasn't a regular hunting or pocketknife, but looked like something more primitive, something out of a movie about lost tribes. Its handle had the soft brown look of deer antler, and the blade looked viciously sharp, not made of steel but of something more elemental, like obsidian.

"Picked this up in the jungles of Co-Sta-Ree-Co," drawled Luther.

"Blade's as hard and sharp as diamonds. Want me to write a message on your windshield?"

Tod could see, now that Luther held the thing up close to his eyes, that it was in fact a plain fake, molded out of tin and plastic, more likely to have come from a tourist shop in Mexilindo than a jungle.

So this is one chink in the armor, thought Tod. He felt good about that, and he sat up straight at the wheel.

"Be careful with that thing," he said. "Luther, don't do anything to this car, all right? My brother's going to check for every new little scratch when I get back home."

"But," said Luther, flipping the knife back and forth again between his hands, "this here's no ordinary knife. This knife was used for surgery among the Indians down there. It cuts without tearing, cures without blood. I can stick it into anything I want without opening a wound. Watch this!"

And with that Luther suddenly seized the knife in his right hand and plunged it with all his strength into an expanse of white upholstery just an inch from Tod's shoulder. But before Tod could move or speak in outrage, he heard Luther's cackling laugh and saw the joke—it was one of those knives that kids play with, the kind where the blade retracts inside the handle on a spring and makes a pretty good illusion of penetration.

Still enjoying his prank, Luther reached behind him and put the knife away in an outside pocket of his daypack, then turned to face his driver with a grin Tod could feel burning into him without his turning to look.

"Luther, you gave me a scare," sighed Tod, not wanting to laugh, not wanting to approve of such lunacy. But when he stole a glance, Luther was sullen again, staring into his lap, biting his lip, then slipping a finger into his pocket, producing another barrette with which he regathered his ponytail.

"Let me out of here," Luther said quietly, succinctly.

"Why?" cried Tod, alarmed. "Why do you want to get out here in the middle of nowhere?" Then he laughed, condescendingly. "I'm not a murderer, you know. And you couldn't have picked a worse spot, I'm afraid."

"Don't be afraid, man," said Luther, speaking evenly, pleasantly. "Just let me out, this is where I want to get out."

"But hey," replied Tod, not wanting to seem concerned but at the same time reaching with one foot into the darkness beneath the steering wheel and braking the Imperial to a crawl. "This isn't anywhere. It's still a few miles to Rosetta. Let me drive you into town and find a good spot for you to hitch."

But even while he spoke Tod felt secretly relieved, and pulled off the road and finally braked to a complete stop in a swirl of trash. For some reason he turned off his headlights. A moment later Luther had sprung out of the car, had taken a few steps down the ink-dark road, then dashed back to talk to Tod again through the open window.

"Thank you," he breathed, as if having resolved some interior struggle. "I'm okay. You go on to Rosetta. I think I prefer to walk from here, see if some fucker comes along who's maybe going farther than you are."

"Well," hesitated Tod, "if you're sure. Okee doke. At any rate, thanks for the company."

Then the hitchhiker's face, strangely bloated and sad, withdrew a bit but stayed framed in the window for a moment as if on a television screen, with eyes so puppyish and soft in the darkness that Tod suddenly realized that Luther was really as handsome under the beard as a soap-opera star. Then the face disappeared, and Tod pulled back onto the highway, and drove on.

There followed several miles of unrelieved boredom.

"I'll stop at Eskimo's," said Tod, and when he saw the yellow and white sign of the twenty-four-hour franchise, he started thinking hard about the chocolate shake that he knew would calm his nerves and give him that extra boost he needed to finish the dry ice job.

The parking lot was empty, but he pulled in carefully between two of the fishbone parking lines farthest from the door of the restaurant. He was thinking so hard about the shake that he had almost put the episode of the hitchhiker out of his mind, and so it was with a wrench of astonishment and sorrow that he noticed that Luther had forgotten his green daypack. There it was, still nestled among the misty ice blocks, a remnant of the vagabond, a sliver that he couldn't get out of his finger. The thing to do, he considered, was to dump the thing in the garbage and get on to the market.

Or leave it in the parking lot where Luther might find it?

It was just then that he saw the girl. She was tiny and bright, a Tinkerbelle, maybe fourteen years old, or fifteen. She appeared to him first through the rear window of the Imperial, but distant, a little figure far across the parking lot, standing at the entrance to the restaurant. She was wearing a white and yellow cap that from where he sat looked like a giant fried egg, and she was holding open the restaurant door from the inside and calling out to him.

"I was just thinking of closing," he could barely hear her shout at him, in a crackling but immediately appealing voice. "Did you want something to eat here or to go?"

"I thought—" he cried back after a second, after he had scrambled out of the car and stood up on the door ledge to get a better look at her. "I thought all Eskimo's were open twenty-four hours."

"Yeah, I know," she yelled, and started walking across the parking lot toward him. "It's just that I'm working alone tonight. I've been cooped up in there for more hours than I care to think about and I was thinking about saying screw the customers—excuse me, of course I don't mean you—and, you know, sneaking out."

She stopped about ten feet away and Tod saw that her cap was supposed to look not like an egg but like a daisy. "But come on if you'd like," she smiled.

Then, because of the daypack, Tod faced a decision. He could drive back and try to find the hitchhiker, or he could go in and eat and assume that the hitchhiker might find his way to Eskimo's and recognize the Carluxe.

"OK," said the girl, taking some steps backward. "I hereby take your silence to mean no. OK? We're closed. Sorry we missed you. Come back and see us again soon."

"No, no," said Tod, suddenly fishing out the daypack, slinging it over one shoulder, and taking a few steps toward her. "I want a Polar Bear Burger," he lied, feeling less hungry than before. There was a thin sharp smell of cattle manure in the air, almost like a mist, and he remembered the big Rosetta feedlots. "I want fries and I want a chocolate shake. To go. I'll eat it in my car, and then you can close up."

But she was already on her way back to the restaurant and he had to run to slip inside the automatic glass door as it closed just behind her.

Inside the restaurant everything was as bright as noon in the basin, but compared to the outside heat, absurdly cold, and all the walls and tables and chairs were covered in crisp, phosphorescent tones of yellow, white, and green. No customers in sight. After a few minutes the girl brought the food, not packaged to go, to Tod's table and then, to his surprise, sat down across from him and watched quietly while he ate.

At first he concentrated on the food. He was interested to find, upon unfastening the Styrofoam clamshell that he expected to contain his sandwich, a pile of steaming, garlicky shrimp. But he said nothing, made no complaint. The rest of the food was as he had ordered: a tall round waxy cup, with its charge of chocolate shake, too thick to sip through the clear plastic straw. There, too, was the order of fries, cut in half-moon shapes that reminded him, when they spilled out of their bag on the bright table in the bright green light, more of lime wedges than potatoes.

The girl's face, as he ate, followed his movements, and was so bright and round that it distracted him. But, he thought to himself as he jostled the last bit of shake into his mouth and shot a glance over the edge of the cup, she is not especially attractive. Her face is round and smooth, he thought, but she is not a beautiful girl, she could not be hired as a model. For one thing she didn't have enough hair; instead of cascading to her shoulders or streaming out like ripples of summer wheat, her locks hung straight and limp beneath her hat, like Luther's. She had brought the food to him wearing, suddenly, an oversized school jacket decorated not with athletic letters but with several little enameled pins that he decided must be academic awards, and now he noticed her habit, whenever she lay her arms on the table, of clenching her fists and drawing them just inside the frayed sleeves, two instant amputations. That's not becoming, he said to himself, and also he didn't like her eyes, which were small and black, eyelashes done with mascara in a way, he thought, that made them look more like a pair of black stitches in her face than eyes.

"Why is it always so unbearably cold in here?" she said out loud suddenly, wrapping her handless arms around her ribs. She shook her head no and leaned forward when she spoke.

"You're asking me?" snorted Tod, toying with his final french fry, not looking up.

"It's the manager, he keeps the air-conditioner controls under lock and key, so we can't set the temperature to something a little more realistic. He says the tourists like it this way. But guess what?"

"What?"

"They complain to me about it all the time."

She shook her head no and leaned forward again, and Tod realized that this was a kind of tic with her, her odd way of speaking. He thought it gave her conversation a strange quality of conspiracy, and he tried to chew quietly as she talked because he wanted to hear every word. Then, when she was quiet for a long time, he swallowed and spoke. "And you can't open the doors to warm things up," he suggested, "because of the feedlots."

"Very true. It isn't surprising that customers don't want to think about feedlots too much when they're inhaling their ground beef. But now we'll talk about *your* interesting job."

"What makes you think I've got an interesting job? Or that there is such a thing?"

"I don't know. You have an interesting job because you strike me as mature enough for an interesting job. Either that or you go to college at India Basin, where I go, or up in Santa Sierra. Or even in Brahma. You grew up here on the lake. You work during the summers and live with your parents."

Tod ate his last fry, then began carefully and idly to fold the greasy cardboard shell that read "french fries" in murderously red letters.

"Hey," he said. "How can you just slip out, like you said you were going to? Doesn't the manager come around to check on you?"

"He comes every morning at five—he's very predictable. I know how to get back just in time and make it look like I've been here. But—hey yourself—I really do want to know about your job."

He paused, then lied. She had said his job must be interesting, and Tod lied only to keep from shattering the atmosphere which he felt all around them and which he knew her flattery had made.

"My brother and I run an ice factory. We inherited it from our dad. That's my job. I mostly do the delivery side of the business."

"Do you really have ice in that car? Why doesn't it melt?"

"The way they—we—wrap it up with paper, it melts very slowly. But besides that it's dry ice."

"Do you have a boss? Is he like mine?"

"It's my brother."

"Your brother is your boss?"

"No. You don't get it. We run the business together. He's more like my partner. But he takes care of the plant, and I make the deliveries."

Tod was watching the girl as he spoke, wondering what her name was, but it seemed too late already to ask. Her face, he kept thinking, was so round. Nice and round. Round like an Eskimo's.

"All right," she said, frowning, shaking. "Now for the hardest question. What kind of contraband are you carrying in the bag?"

But the bag, Luther's daypack, was something Tod had already forgotten about, and for a moment he was startled and couldn't imagine what she was talking about.

"Oh that," he finally shrugged. "That's a funny story. I picked up a hitchhiker on the way here and he forgot it in my truck."

"But that's too good to be true!" the girl screeched. The frown was broken, and she laughed and clapped her hands, then held her hands in front of her nose like a closed book while Tod stirred uncomfortably on his plastic bench seat. "Do you realize," she smiled, "who you picked up?"

"No idea," he mumbled, half-expecting her to say that it was her fiancé or her boyfriend and thus break the spell.

"The vanishing hitchhiker, that's who. You don't know the story? All right, the story goes like this. You're driving late one night on Highway 7, say, and you pick up a solitary figure at the side of the road. He introduces himself, you introduce yourself, you proceed to have a nice conversation. Maybe he makes cryptic remarks about a car crash, maybe he doesn't. At any rate you let him off, only to discover later that he's left something in your car, maybe a wallet, maybe a DAYPACK. Anyway, it has to be something with his address in it. You find the address, notice it's in a nearby town, and drive over the next day to return the forgotten item. Except the hitchhiker doesn't answer the doorbell, it's his wife or his mother. You tell her the story and all the while she's looking at you like you're crazy or she's just seen a ghost. 'But that's impossible,' she says. 'Our Herbert died in an auto accident a year ago yesterday.' 'Where exactly was the accident?' you ask, an icy hand laying hold of your heart. 'Why, right out on Highway 7,' she says, 'JUST OUTSIDE OF GIZA BEACH.'"

Tod was unimpressed. "This was not one of your ghost hitchhikers," he said. "Besides, he wasn't from around here, he was from Texas."

"Oh," the girl snapped, impatient, drawing her hands even farther into her sleeves. "You don't get it, do you? The next thing I was going to say is, let's look inside his daypack, for an address, go look up the poor fellow's family."

"My story's more interesting than that, because it's a true story."
At the same time that he spoke Tod was comparing Luther and the
girl, thinking how much he had been getting to like her, how much
more he would rather tell her some more stories. Maybe the one
about the ammonia leak, just to get things started. Then he would
settle back and listen to her for a while, and maybe, he thought, learn
a thousand things from her, let her be his real teacher. But then she
had spoiled things by talking about ghosts.

On the other hand. What if her story were true?

Meanwhile the girl was grimacing and biting the knuckle of her
index finger in such a way that it had turned red and white and shiny,
like a gnawed bone. "Listen," she said. "I wonder. Well I wonder if
you could do me a favor while you're here."

Tod hesitated. Suddenly he had run out of words, suddenly he was
dull and nervous and feeling the dryness of the air conditioner in his
sinuses, and he daubed at his nostril with his finger, and it came away
with a perfect little bead of blood. In the silence he started thinking
about making love to the girl, about what it would be like. He pictured
her, for some reason, wearing a black bra, like tough high school girls
wear, and wondered if it would be the kind that undid in the front or
the back. Then he had a terrible image of himself trying to penetrate
her, but with a penis that retracted with every thrust, like Luther's
knife.

"I wonder if you could do me a big favor," repeated the girl, leaning
forward across the table and opening her miniature, all-black eyes as
wide as they could go.

"What favor?"

"I'd really like to get out for a while. But now it's gotten so late. I
wonder if you could stay here in case the manager comes along.
Could you? If he comes in while I'm gone, just say that I had to go
around to the bathroom. Then come outside to the date garden and
whistle or something. Will you?"

"There's a date garden?"

"Yeah. You didn't know? We're surrounded by palm trees here,
it's nice. You didn't see the palms? This is the old Vern-Lee Gardens.
This used to be Vern-Lee's Date Shack before they turned it into an

Eskimo's. Anyway, when you came that's just where I was heading, I mean, into the garden. Every night I try to get out and take a long walk out there—it's really pretty great at night. Kind of spooky, you know? If I don't get to do it I just about don't make it to the end of my shift. Will you do it? Will you cover for me?"

Tod could hardly wait for her to stop talking, he was so prepared with his answer. "Yes," he said intently, leaning a little toward her. "Yes."

"I don't know. Are you sure? Maybe I'll get you in trouble with your job? Are you sure your ice won't melt?"

"It won't melt. Anyway, what if I told you it wasn't ice after all, that I'd been lying about everything? That what I have in the back of the car isn't ice, but the body of that hitchhiker, that I've killed him and brought him here to bury in the date garden?"

The girl looked upset for a moment and then she broke into a great round Eskimo grin.

"That's better," she laughed. "That's great. When I get back we'll check that daypack of yours and get the family address."

"OK. See you."

And she was gone, dancing out into the night, leaving a puff of feedlot air behind her as the glass door closed without a sound. Tod stretched his legs out on the bench, leaned back against the softness of Luther's pack, and then, serenely, trustingly, fell asleep.

The first thing he realized when he woke up was that he was still alone in Eskimo's, and the second thing he realized was that the sun was starting to come up, and that there was a piece of paper on the table that hadn't been there before and that it was in fact a letter meant for him.

Dear customer (ice delivery man):
Thanks again for being here while I went out. I did come back a few minutes later to ask you something but you were asleep. What I wanted to ask was can Luther and I borrow your car, but didn't want to wake you up so took your keys anyway and promise we'll be very careful with your fine car and your ice and just be gone a short while. Sorry I kidded you about Luther. That business about the vanishing hitchhiker was just my stupid joke. The minute you walked in I knew you had given Luther a ride because I recognized his green daypack. Luther is, as I guess you

can figure out, really my boyfriend, and I guess he kidded you too when he told you he doesn't live around here. The real reason I had to leave you alone was to meet him. Don't worry we'll be back before sunrise and before customers start showing up. Yours, the Eskimo's girl (Janine).

Still slow with sleep and recoiling from the gritty, shrimpy taste in his teeth, Tod rose, stuffed the letter in a pocket, and swung Luther's daypack onto his right shoulder. When he stumbled out into the parking lot he found the predawn wind not just free of heat and feedlot misery, but full, for just a moment, of a strange winter sweetness and coolness. He gladly breathed it in, like a diver who comes up from holding his breath too long, and as he breathed, and even as the coolness disappeared and was replaced by the familiar suffocation, his eyes cleared and he felt the creases relax a little in his face, even in his clothes. The first thing he looked for in the rising light was the date garden, and when he turned instinctively in the direction of the refreshing wind, he saw for the first time the tall feathery outlines of palm fronds silhouetted against the gray sky, already alive with the sound of tiny, nervous birds who hid themselves high up in the deep black-green of the foliage. There, he said to himself, is my oasis, and he had taken several long, unimaginably buoyant steps toward the trees when he was brought up short by the belated realization that what the letter said was true, that Ike's car, the vermilion Carluxe, was gone.

Tod hissed. I'm not responsible for this, he thought, I'm not to blame, no one can blame me for this. I kept Luther from wrecking the car before but this loss is a result of something insane, something I can't control. Suddenly he sat down hard on the asphalt, his back turned to the dates, facing the glaring yellow light of Eskimo's. I'll wait for them here, he thought, and play it cool. Nevertheless, he couldn't help bringing his hand down hard on the black asphalt, holding back a sob, spitting out something. Then, acting on a different impulse, he jumped up, wheeled around, and set out for the date garden.

Tod realized it must be one of the old gardens that had been planted decades ago, back when there was some odd idea that the valley could become the date-growing capital of the world, could surpass the ancient cultivations of India and Egypt. For a while, his brother had told him, the harvests were impressive and the soft heavy dates were superior quality, and there was a lot of excitement and planning. But soon most of the trees had succumbed to a mysterious tree rot and died, aliens from another desert, unable to adapt. Years later a few diminished groves remained in the valley, some providing fruit for curious tourists, others, like this one, neglected, losing their sweet crop every year to the lucky birds. Tod, for one, had never paid much attention to the orchards, never even eaten the good sweet dates at harvest time. Now, as he walked down the corridors formed by the smooth silver trunks and could watch the sun just emerging at the end of the perpendicular corridors to his left, Tod felt larger than life, like a holy man in some cathedral of Islam, wading thoughtfully through the thick grass that grew between the marblelike columns, falling to his knees once to examine the bright drops of dew and tiny yellow flowers that turned out to be not flowers but tiny yellow pinfeathers the date birds were shedding from above. The thin, sweet breeze that he had swallowed in the parking lot now came to him again. Then it was gone, and the sun was above the horizon and it was miserably hot. He stood up and the birds he had heard before had begun to flutter more noisily, as if agitated by the heat, pitching and scratching at one another loudly, battling for perches in the jungle of fronds twenty or thirty feet above his head. Shifting Luther's daypack on his shoulder, Tod veered sideways into a new long row of trees—and then thought he caught a glimpse of red quite far away, a shade of reddish orange that made him think that it had to be his brother's car.

Tod moved cautiously to his right, and there in fact it was, the Carluxe, only now it was directly ahead of him, in full view, parked in sunlight, windows rolled up tight, grass shivering around the hubcaps. He stepped slowly toward it, dull with fear, following the wounds in the grass left by the tires. Now he could feel absolutely no further pleasure in the burning morning. The sun, though only an inch above the horizon, had already begun to scorch the tops of his bare forearms and fill his throat, as on every summer day in the basin, with the taste of syrup, of yellow solar expectorant.

There was no farther to go. He could reach forward and pull open the passenger door if he wanted, but he hesitated. He did try to open the door, but it was locked. Then, running a hand along the long strip of cool chrome trim, he walked slowly around the whole circumference of the Imperial, idly swallowing down the heat like soda pop, finding all the doors locked tight.

Not that he could see in. It was all opaque because the dry ice, in its slow disintegration, had filled the whole interior of the car with fog. Tod considered the fog, and decided on two likely explanations for it. One was that Luther and Janine were nearby—he pictured them rolling together in a patch of sweet grass—and had left the windows rolled up when they left the car.

The other possibility was that the couple—the two, he kept thinking, who had lied to him—were still in the car. If they were in the car—and Tod considered this possibility with a stab of satisfaction, followed by a flood of melancholy—they were dead, asphyxiated. Slowly, composedly, he considered how he might get inside the car and free them, revive them, and he even rummaged for a second in the daypack, hoping to find some kind of tool or wire. But of course the only thing that he came up with was the toy knife, which was useless. Maybe, he thought, staring again, taking a step backward, maybe Janine and Luther had really believed that they might flee the wretched heat by rolling up the windows and letting the ice air-condition their love. But it was dry ice, as he was sure he had told one or both of them, again and again, and it was truly cold, colder than cold, but poison.

Thing
One
and
Thing
Two

───────────

Catalina was only fifteen, and innocent, but every night since her family's move down to Mexico she had suffered from intense insomnia, a sleeplessness more appropriate to the elderly, or the condemned.

Lying face up, the hot sheets cast aside, her body as flat and delicate as a fallen leaf, she found that the only way to fumble toward sleep was to write a kind of science fiction story in her head.

It usually was this: she imagined herself scuba diving in the oceans of an ocean planet, descending through ever murkier fathoms of poisoned waters.

Sometimes this worked.

More often she needed to imagine further than that, and she had to go on and dream herself precipitating toward the deck of a certain sunken spacecraft, a black and alien thing that her imagination had constructed in fine detail and which resembled, she realized with a trace of pride, an Art Nouveau submarine, a Jules Verne kind of thing. There, standing on top of the craft, she would slowly—so slowly!—unscrew an ancient iron door, then float down into an interior as dark and suffocating as boiled ink. Then sleep. If that worked.

But if that didn't work, if she still couldn't sleep after that, she'd allow herself to float farther down into the cockpit and place her dream hand on the throttlelike control. Sliding the mechanism forward, she would carefully guide the spacecraft down through sheer seabed and down, like a ghost, through the bituminous rock, setting a course for the distant center of the world.

Of course there were nights when even that didn't work—nights when she would travel all the way to the frozen core and have no farther to go but still lie there awake, all sweaty and electric. On the hottest nights of the year she'd simply sigh and sigh again into the same space of air just above her mouth, dangling a slender arm between the bed and the wall but otherwise perfectly still in her white pajamas, staring at the blue blinking digits of the clock radio and reflecting on the probable, even certain existence of beings so advanced that they—but were they beings from the future or from the past?—had done away with sleep altogether and replaced it with all-night mental competitions and pure intellectual gymnastics.

This was in the north of Mexico, in the state of Sonora, where in summer people talking on the streets wouldn't compare the weather to an oven but to the inside of a light bulb. Each morning at Cat's house there finally would come, at dawn, through her open window, a blast of new light, a touch of breeze. Then, because the first hour was the coolest of the day, she would get up, sit in the chair by the window, stare out toward the distant stacks of the power plants, sip in whatever thread of coolness she might find in the morning air, and finally, her arms on the windowsill and her head in her arms, fall asleep in such a way that her thin blonde ponytail hung out raggedly over the sill like the tail of an angry yellow feline.

One morning during what seemed like the hottest summer of all, the summer that Catalina finished the ninth grade, she emerged from her bedroom to find that the JayBee Scientific Supply catalog, ordered so long ago she had forgotten all about it, had finally arrived in the mail. The book lay on the floor in the hallway where her mom or her dad had left it for her to see, and when she picked it up it was thick and heavy, like the Los Angeles Yellow Pages she had once read cover to cover as a child. She sat down suddenly on the floor of the hall and opened it, and there in the half-darkness tried to make out the contents of thousands of small grainy photos printed on newsprint. It seemed that JayBee had put in a picture of everything: instruments, models, cases, meters, glass vials, mounted specimens, live animals, frozen organs, toxic compounds, knives, needles, pins. Cat wanted all of it, then half of it, then only the sea hares in formaldehyde and the dissecting microscope, both of which, on reflection, she rejected.

Then, on the very last page of the book, there was a submarine for sale. Just as in her insomnia, it floated up to meet her from the page, black as a foul cigar, a military discard, an American flag impossibly unfurled underwater, screw-down hatches set solidly into the deck. Gulf of Tonkin Veteran, read the ad copy. Ready for oceanographic refitting.

She tore out that page and memorized it as carefully as she might a chemistry test, except that she unconsciously altered the price in her mind from $95,000 to $9,500. Every night she would lie under a single hot sheet with a flashlight, the way some girls do to read their Brontë or Judy Blume, only that she had no book, only the memory, projected onto the white sheet, of the grainy photograph of the submarine. Cat would chew her lip and keep thinking that there must be some way for her to buy it. She was young and financially ignorant but imagined she could get a job.

She had never had a job. She felt certain that in Mexico they paid you a lot less than in the States, but she knew they would have to pay her something.

But here was another plan: she could wait for one of those periods, not infrequent, when her parents were disgusted with each other, were not speaking to each other, and exploit that. Tell her mother that her father had hit her, and now she needed money for a psychiatrist. Tell her dad that Mom wanted some money so that she and Cat could get away from him for a while. Then she would send in the money, and they would deliver the submarine, deliver it right to her door, and there it would be, sitting on the front curb, frightening the neighbors and motel guests with its matte-black hull and towering, prying periscope. The "oceanographic refitting" would somehow be accomplished, and then she would make it her mission to explore the bottom of the nearby laguna. Not melodramatically, not with a great moral mission, not like Captain Nemo, she thought. And not, like some bad, silly child, to escape her parents' scrutiny. No. Simply to make a useful survey, she told herself. Simply to note salinity levels, note forms of life, even discover new species and varieties, return with photographs and data. Write a book. Get a Ph.D. All without going to the university in Mexico City, where her father wanted her to go. At last this daydream faded a little. Finally, more realistically, more economically—but still taking up all the bills she had crammed like socks in the back of her drawer—she ended up going back to the catalog and ordering a box of "Mojave Geodes." A magic crystal world, it read, is revealed to the delight of you and your friends. Please allow nine weeks for delivery.

Geodes were interesting. She had never had any in her mineral collection, but a few weeks earlier the word had come up in a conversation with a boy and when she saw them in the catalog she remembered the conversation and decided she might very much like to have a few of her own. It had happened like this: a boy she barely knew had come up to her in the school hallway and clumsily pressed into her hand a book called *La idioma de las flores*. Thumbing through it quickly, casually, she saw how it purported to explain the various moral and romantic meanings of certain flowers. Peonies, for example, on page three, stood for simple honesty, while daisies represented (and here the boy had crudely circled the words with a black marker) "un amor que crezca sin compensación." But Cat had no patience for either the book or the boy, whose name was Humberto and whom she comically addressed from then on as Dumberto. What meanings would there be, she asked him later, serious and scornful, when the flowers were not in bloom? Then she laughed, falsely and pretentiously, and told Humberto that he or better someone else should write a similar book, better for all seasons, all eras, called *The Language of Minerals*.

"Borax," she told him, speaking her fluent Spanish but putting on a comically thick American accent, ignoring the tears that had started in his eyes, "could stand for cleanliness, and coal for hardening of the heart. And geodes—do you know what a geode is, Dumberto? One of those rocks that have the crystals inside when you break them open? Geodes could stand, couldn't they, tonto, for, oh, rip you off, or, oh, fake you out."

Cat's father looked a little bit like her. But there were, at least in her mind, key differences. For example, where she had white and slender hands, with fingers like weeds, he had little dark hands, leather hands, like a handball player or a dirt farmer. Unlike most hands, the palms were darker than the tops, a detail that was sometimes hidden in embarrassed fists, sometimes held up to general comment and examination. Many years before he had worked as a shoeshine boy in the capital of his native South American country, and he liked to say that that was how he got such dark palms, from the gallons of boot black and a decade of hard work in those bright equatorial plazas. But, immigrating north with his parents, he had spent the second half of his childhood in Giza Beach, gone to high school there, and married Penny Fleetwood from Thermal. Later, after Cat was born, her father started talking more and more about moving across the border, to where he claimed the schools were tougher and more disciplined, and when Cat was ten he bought a motel in Mexilindo, the kind where each unit is a separate cottage and the front office connects to the owner's house. It was named the Tres Paises, because from the top of a nearby mountain you were supposed to be able to see three countries: Mexico, the U.S., and a little Mormon town a few miles away that had proclaimed itself an independent nation.

Cat proceeded to subject herself to the very strict and unbearable schools her father had dreamed of, but it was too late; she had spent too many semesters in the relaxed and rebellious atmosphere of Los Angeles schools and never succeeded in thinking with the unruffled actuality of a Mexican, of an insider. When her Mexican teachers and counselors asked her what she wanted to be when she grew up, she told them that she already was something. That she was a science fiction writer.

The catalog said nine weeks, and nine weeks to the day after she placed her order a brown, battered delivery van with California plates pulled up at the curb in front of the motel. By then the weather had turned from scalding to merely hot, and Cat ran out to greet the van wearing jeans, a heavy tweed overcoat, and the hat she always wore, a khaki thing like they wear in the French Foreign Legion, with a long brim and desert flaps hanging down over the neck and ears. The driver shouldered open a sliding side door and then, with a magician's snap of the quilted shipping blanket, revealed a cubical wooden box about the size of a family television and painted red. Cat impulsively leapt inside the dark, mildew-fragrant interior of the van to help the driver unload—only to find that it wasn't allowed, that the guy was a squinting and solemn Chicano with a Hell's Angel mustache, the kind of cholo turned respectable worker who couldn't stand customers who fussed and watched and tried to help.

"See this?" he said to Cat in English, extending his arm toward her to show her a tattoo printed on top of his fist. Though it was dark inside the van she could make out, just above the knuckles, the words "El Alma Herido" surrounded by little yellow daisies. "You know Spanish? That's Spanish for 'Leave the merchandise alone.' You know what a slogan is? Companies have slogans, like 'You deserve a break today,' and this here is my slogan."

"Well, here's mine," returned Cat, glaring, holding out a lapel button she had been fingering in her pocket but couldn't bring herself to wear. It read, "Where in Hell is Calilindo?"

Later, alone in the yard in front of the motel, Cat embraced her new box, pressing her nose into the sweet paint smell, trying without success to lift the whole thing by herself, not because it was so heavy but because she could barely get her arms around it. It was beautiful to look at. Because it was painted red and had a large metal hook holding down the lid, the box looked to her like the one the Cat in the Hat opens in order to let loose on the world his funny and ultra-destructive friends, Thing One and Thing Two.

When she ceremoniously undid the latch she thought she would find a naked pile of geodes, but instead there was a bundle of black, tar-covered paper that peeled off in sticky sheets, and peeled off, and peeled off, until she wondered in despair if there would be any geodes inside at all. Finally she got to a layer of wax paper, and then a layer of newspaper, and when that was ripped off she finally had two geodes the size of baseballs. She sat down with them sullenly and cautiously rolled them back and forth across her palms.

"Thing One and Thing Two," she smiled, feeling horrible and

ripped off because there were only two and they were not at all attractive, although she knew you were supposed to crack them open to see the wonderland of crystals on the inside. She wasn't sure when or if she would do it, but she could picture herself whirling a hammer over her head with the grace of a ballerina, then suddenly striking Thing One and Thing Two and laying open an interior of crystals—crystals that in their explosion and dispersion would whisper to her of something, she was not sure what. The only words that came to mind were rhyming words that made no sense: sentimental, sedimental, elemental, detrimental. She whistled as she tossed the halves of the rock up and down in her hand. Fundamental, instrumental, excremental.

Why not make up new mentals, she thought. Gentlemental, lamentamental. Locomental?

She wondered if she should send them back. Should she pass them out to friends at school? She had no friends at school. Should she start her own geode business? There were only two, but that might be enough to make a little money by hiding them in the desert and leading some tourists out on a bogus rockhound adventure.

The next morning she stuffed some things in a backpack—a few candy bars, a thermos of coffee, and, wrapped in newspaper again, the two treasures—and walked a little way into the desert, halfway up the scrubby, yellow slope of Cerro de Salpetre. She didn't know why she felt compelled to go there, because she didn't know enough about the origin of geodes. Were they typically found on the surface, for example, or buried deep down? But somehow Cerro de Salpetre seemed like a spot where people who had been told they could find geodes in the desert would go to find geodes. It was, after all, a terrain littered with all sorts of debris: clumps of rock, scraps of rusted metal refuse, strange fragments of plaster blown in from the distant figurines factory, shreds of toilet paper that clung to cactus spines. Why not a geode here and there to spice things up? They would all, Cat was sure, enjoy finding geodes.

She was not surprised, then, when, after putting up a notice in the lobby, she immediately got her first customers, two elderly ladies staying in room 29.

Later, after she had taken the ladies out and returned home in triumph, she was so pleased with herself that she went to look for

Penny, her mother, and tell her how she had made enough money from the excursion to pay for both geodes, and she still had one of them left.

While Penny sat behind the registration desk cutting out magazine pictures for her decoupage, Cat leaned against the magazine rack, the brim of her hat pulled low, telling the story of her day as she pulled out magazines at random, thumbed through the pictures and put them back, and helped herself to cup after cup from the coffee maker that sat dripping and steaming near the window in a square of dirty late summer light.

"When I saw the look on that old Mrs. Banning's face," said Cat, ending her story, "the whole thing was worth it just for that. Her look was absolutely detrimental. I could have started up my business just for that, and then quit."

Cat spoke over the rim of her cup, the corners of her mouth stretched into a careless imitation of Mrs. Banning's ecstasy—the grin, enlarged with orange lipstick, that had lit the old lady's face at that moment when she thought she had found a geode all by herself. After Cat had smashed it with the crowbar, Mrs. Banning flourished the three or four glittering fragments over her head, a show of exultation for the benefit of her friend, a very quiet, very suntanned snowbird who had worried Cat the whole morning.

"Mrs. Banning's friend, on the other hand," Cat continued, serious now, twirling the Styrofoam cup in her hands to get at a lump of undissolved cream powder, "she was too stupid to get excited about finding a real geode. But old Mrs. Banning. She's just great. While we're coming back she keeps going, 'They're just gorgeous, they're just gorgeous.' Like I'd helped her find some diamonds or something."

"Don't," Penny whispered.

But Cat didn't hear, or choose to hear, and went on chattering.

"Right now I bet both those old snowbirds are over there in twenty-nine studying the darn thing. Even as we speak, they're going, ooh, aah, won't Harry back in Bismarck think this is a great paperweight."

"Don't, don't!" Penny yelled, apparently furious, though she continued to methodically snip at a picture in the magazine, using, Cat noticed with surprise, a pair of children's scissors that had once been hers.

Thing One and Thing Two   43

"Right now," she continued, "I am not in a mood to be aggravated. Right now, I am not in any mood to be entertained with stories about you and your harebrained geodes."

At that moment, however, it was not that Penny was so angry about the geodes—although the bald dishonesty of it all did not appeal to her—as she was about the gray and scratchy wool coat, huge and hanging loose, no buttons, that Cat wore on her rock-hunting tours, the overcoat that she wore to make herself, as she always told her parents, look more mature, more businesslike.

"I'm going to take it off in a second," she frowned, seeing the way her mother looked at the coat and for once somewhat understanding her, feeling sorry for her. The coat, after all, had been salvaged from the trunk of her father's car, where it had been used to cover a spare tire. Now it had a raspberry jam smell from stains of transmission fluid on the broad, old-fashioned lapels. The perspiration she gave off while wearing the thing with only a tee shirt underneath in the warm afternoons, while her clients followed along in shorts, sandals, and tank tops, felt pleasantly sharp and tingling at certain points of her body, as if, at just those points, she were sweating Alka Seltzer. The hat came from Los Angeles.

But there, in the motel lobby, pouring another cup of coffee in the silence that followed Penny's outburst, she concentrated on something she had never concentrated on before: how she could please her mother. Finally she shrugged off the heavy overcoat and let it fall to the floor. Then, light as a feather without it, she spun around, spilling the coffee a little, making the flaps of the legionnaire's hat whirl out like a figure skater's skirt. It worked. Penny laughed, and then they both laughed at how agile Cat was, at what a magical, happy difference taking the coat off had made for both of them.

Hours later, just before dark, they were still there. Penny had gone back to her magazines and her daughter had put her coat back on, not slipping her arms through the satin-lined sleeves, but draping the whole weight of it over her shoulders like an older, more sophisticated woman. The black telephone at her mother's elbow, which all afternoon Cat had expected to ring with another request for a geode excursion, was quiet. Then Penny, with a heavy sigh, but without putting aside her magazine, reached under the counter and slid an unopened box of pencils toward where her daughter was still sipping coffee and staring out the window.

"Do me a favor, honey, and sharpen these up?"

Cat was silent.

"Cat, honey, you know we'll need these later for the new ledgers and such, and to give out to the guests."

"I don't know where the sharpener is," said Cat, suddenly lunging to the counter and grabbing the pencils.

"Sorry, but I do. Hey, don't huff off like that."

"Where?" called Cat from the kitchen.

"It's in the drawer with the maps," Penny called back, but Cat had already found it and had sat down at the kitchen table, with her coat still slung over her shoulders and the pencils and sharpener laid out before her. She hadn't wanted to turn the lights on, and the only illumination for her job came from the street light that had just come on out on the highway.

They were blue #3 pencils with the name of the motel stamped in gold. The sharpener was an old thing that had been drifting from drawer to drawer for years, ever since Cat was a baby. It was round, about the size of a Ping-Pong ball, and painted or lithographed into a globe of the world. The continents were there in their different colors, and a handful of cities, but for some reason, maybe because it was so small, the manufacturer had not included national borders, so that the little globe seemed to symbolize a kind of tattered global unity. Cat held the somewhat scratched and battered sphere up in the fluorescent glare that poured in through the window.

This is how the earth would appear to the colonists on Mars, she thought. Through the telescopes they'll see that it looks just like a banged-up old pencil sharpener; they'll see that there's an enormous hole where Antarctica used to be, and they won't want to come back.

Slowly, thoughtfully, Cat sharpened, revolving the earth around the tip of every pencil, while Asia, Africa, and America paraded under her twisting and tiring fingers a hundred times. Finally the hollow interior of the globe could hold no more shavings, and with one foot she pulled the kitchen trashcan toward her, then pried apart the two tin halves and let the wood and lead debris spill out. But here was a surprise. At the bottom of the trashcan she discovered the good kitchen scissors. They had been thrown away, or hidden away, with their handles—but not the blades—taped closed. That was what was strangest of all: the fact that someone had gone to the trouble of taking black electrician's tape and winding yards and yards of it around the handles, slowly building up the layers of tape to form an ugly lumpy handle almost too thick to get her hand around. It was as if someone had been trying to make the scissors into a dagger.

Cat didn't dare to pick up the thing, but instead silently finished the pencils and made a point of letting the shavings fall in such a way as to gradually powder over and disguise and erase from her mind the sight of the unimaginable weapon.

But she couldn't erase it. Half an hour passed, and she still sat motionlessly and thought hard, but could not solve the mystery of the taped-up scissors, except to conclude that if she were to ask Penny or her father about them, she would likely be pressured into taking sides in yet another of their ongoing disputes.

"So forget it," she said aloud. "Let's just fucking forget it. Leave the merchandise alone."

She realized, with a light touch to her mouth, that her lips were badly chapped, and the realization brought her back to her senses. She could tell that Penny was still sitting at the counter because she could hear her still snipping pictures out of magazines, and finally she walked out in the brightly lit lobby to deliver the pencils.

"You took an awfully long time," said Penny. "I could hear you sharpening pencils, and then I couldn't hear you doing anything for a long time."

"Mom," said Cat, "what's that a picture of?"

Penny held up the clipping and stared at it hard, as if to think about it harder than ever before, as if to try and penetrate for once why she would spend her time cutting out such things and gluing them down on slices of wood, then later pouring resin over everything and sometimes getting Cat's father to drill a hole and insert some clock hands on the front and a little battery-run clock motor in the back. This time the clipping was a drawing of an old table-top radio, with an aproned mother and ringleted little girl angled joyfully over it, and Penny had clipped it so as to follow the outlines of the figures and the radio and leave out the background.

"What do you think?" she asked finally and held it against one of her decoupage tablets, an oval slice of redwood with the bark still attached. "Doesn't the little girl look like you when you were a baby? I could have the clock hands come out of the radio, and when it was five to one the big hand would point to the mom and the little hand would point to the little girl."

"It's OK," answered Cat. "Mom, why are you using my old scissors?"

But there was no chance for her mother to answer. Just then Mrs. Banning marched in from the parking lot, slamming the door as she came, and stood breathing heavily in the middle of the lobby, looking back and forth from Cat to her mother, her eyes swollen with what seemed like a mixture of triumph and bewilderment. Cat could tell that Mrs. Banning was about to say something enormous, though at first she could not imagine that it might have anything to do with her.

Then suddenly Mrs. Banning, still speechless and still wide-eyed, was coming at her, coming at Cat, holding the two halves of her geode over her head in such a way that the two cups of crystal were full of brilliant, almost mystical light and Cat thought of her for a second as someone somehow religious, an angel directing beams of light toward the earth. But the elderly woman's thick and dimpled upper arms had turned red with heat rash, her lips were twisted in accusation. Somehow—perhaps because she had checked her geode in a book, perhaps because she had been persuaded by her friend—she had formed some idea of Cat's little deception, and now the speech came, and it was all to scold and revile Cat in a high gritty voice that made Cat feel a little sick but at the same time laugh to herself because it was a voice that made her think of a nagging cartoon wife like Wilma Flintstone or, from an older black and white cartoon she had always liked, a little spider wife who nagged her spider husband when he came home without a fly.

"But it's not her fault," cried Penny from behind the counter, throwing back her shoulders, intervening, stamping her feet. "Her father put her up to it. It's her goddamned father who teaches her how to cheat."

Cat's father was broad-chested, a weight lifter, dark skin tough as Naugahyde, born in South America, in the deserts of Peru. Everyone called him, at his own request, The Inca. His voice, especially in Spanish—as good as Chuck Yeager's, or Humberto Luna's people said—was meant for radio. Instead, he set himself up as a mobile advertiser for his other business, his hardware store, with two directional loudspeakers bolted to the roof of his car. It was a job he could have given to some employee, some kid, but he had admired the mobile announcers in his South American childhood, and it represented to him a triumph that he had not only risen from befuddled immigrant to small businessman but was confident enough to be his own spokesman as well. Nevertheless, as he drove he often became sad, daydreaming about the city of his birth and its festooned, stupendous plazas.

"You will see a difference when you try supercharged Dez-Co batteries from Basin Power Automotive." This was one of the messages he blared in Spanish, sometimes in English, driving slowly like an ice cream truck driver through the grid of smoldering summer streets, the blazing hot microphone held close to his lips, everything memorized. In winter, when it rained often, he went out even more often, defying the weather to silence him, and even saying as much through the trumpet-shaped speakers atop the car, which he also used to keep up a little friendly chatter with residents of the small town, broadcasting an occasional hi or how are you or hey say hi to the kids when he drove past certain corners or past the open doors of certain bars.

After the trouble with Mrs. Banning, Penny made Cat give up the geode business, and she started to ride along with The Inca as a semi-salaried employee. One week, as part of a promotional stunt, Cat came along every day, leaning out the car window as they drove and distributing free samples of chlorine powder in little foil packets.

"Don't miss this grand opportunity! All your tool and repair values are just around the corner at Monterrubio Hardware," the speakers blared. "And while you are there, tell them The Inca sent you."

Every afternoon of that week, around four, when the heat had come back to make an uncomfortable Indian summer, Cat's father, without slowing down or pulling over, would take off his shirt, exposing a well-developed torso, a pair of hard pectoral muscles, and a sharply segmented abdomen that reminded Cat, somehow, of upholstery. But when he bared his chest on the third day, on Wednesday, Cat was startled to see a white bandage, in the shape of a triangle, covering a large portion of her father's chest. On the fourth day, Thursday, the bandage was still there, a little dirtier, and The Inca, as he drove, kept picking at it, inserting a nail under the top corner of the pyramid and scratching.

The next week Cat's father asked for help again. This time the plan was to pass out a whole carload of free junior frogman sets. The hardware store wanted to promote its new sporting goods section and so The Inca decided to distribute one hundred packages, each containing a child-size snorkel, a little mask, and a pair of fins, all mounted on colorful cardboard, shrink-wrapped in sparkling clear plastic.

During a break, while they sat in the parked car under a nearly shadeless tree and drank coffee from a thermos, both of them glancing back sometimes at the numerous frogman sets still piled high in the back seat, Cat squirmed on the vinyl seat, her hands deep in the pockets of her wool coat, her khaki brim pulled low. Her father peeled off his damp yellow polo shirt over his head and there once more was the bandage, every corner dog-eared and stained from scratching.

"Too many left," sighed The Inca, using English with his daughter, as was his habit lately. "But I think by now we must have gave one to every kid in the town."

Cat's chin rested on the edge of the rolled-down window. She stared at nothing in particular, breathing in the heavy green smell of weeds around the car. For the first time she felt that she was miserably hot and stupid in her tweed overcoat.

"I will tell you what," continued her father. "Is yours. You can have all these things for you."

"What's mine?" Cat turned her head back to look at her father, but then turned away again when she saw him scratching at the bandage.

"God *damn* this thing," said The Inca. It was the first time he had said a word about it.

"What is that anyway, Dad?" she asked.

Before that moment, Cat hadn't had the courage to bring the subject up. She had imagined her father getting mad in the way he always got mad—gripping the steering wheel as if to pull it out by the roots, turning on the radio to drown out everybody's thoughts, not saying a word until hours later, when the explosion came. But now, now that she did bring it up, now that Cat was able to ask casually about the bandage, The Inca beamed, then frowned, then thrust out his enormous chest like a soldier, as if to show off a medal or a badge.

"That's where your mother she tried to stick me," he announced, like he'd been waiting all that time for that question, speaking in the same musical voice that Cat had grown tired of hearing all morning over the loudspeaker. "You just say thanks God," he continued, "that her scissors was so dull. And that maybe someday this war will get over."

Later Cat helped get rid of the extra sets in the dumpster behind the bait shop. She had already decided not to believe what her father had said about the bandage. The bandage, she figured, was phony— the whole thing had been planned from the start, both her mom and her dad were always taking turns trying to win her sympathy, and this time she wouldn't go along.

"Here's your bonus," said The Inca, frowning, tossing one last snorkel set back into the car. "Hey, you OK?"

Cat was sitting on the ground with her back against the dumpster, clamping her thin hard arms against her stomach.

"I don't want any of those stupid things," she muttered.

"You gotta take it," shrugged her father. "The store wants every kid in town to have one. How's it gonna look if you the only kid without no frogman set?"

"They just seem a little small for me, that's all. And what am I supposed to do with it? What are any of the kids supposed to do with it?"

"OK, Cat in the Hat. Just do this for Daddy, OK? Try it in the bathtub sometime, OK? Anyway, let's go home."

Days later, in a moment of boredom, Cat grabbed the frogman set, tore the plastic shrink wrap off in a frenzy, and took a closer look. The fins, she found, were way too tight on her feet, and she dropped them in the trash. The mask and snorkel, on the other hand, were all right, and she stuck her head out her window, hoping someone would see her wearing them, but there was no one in sight. She lay her head on the sill, let her ponytail hang out into the air, and laughed. "This stupid mask," she said aloud, "will be my submarine." And the next morning she got up early and walked out to the shallow part of the Laguna Ruidosa.

The laguna, once evaporated to almost nothing, to a mud puddle in the middle of a sandy, trash-strewn plain, had swollen a year before from an excess of irrigation and rain and finally sloshed up so close against the streets and residences of Mexilindo that volunteers had been forced to heave hundreds of bags of sand along the beach to build a ragged wall, though not before half of Avenida A had been half-submerged. Cat put on the gear and snorkeled out beyond the sandbag wall, kicking awkwardly through the shallow and transparent water, her hair floating like yellow seaweed around her neck. With the child-size mask cinched a little painfully across her eyes, the snorkel clamped between her teeth with a sweet rubber taste, she drifted out aimlessly, dreamily, angling her legs in a slow frog kick, keeping her arms tight and streamlined against her sides.

She paddled at last through the doorway of an empty old house, its four walls open to the sky. The water sloshed up against shards of broken glass that still stuck to windowpanes. But it was the floor of the house, a few feet under water, that held the snorkeler's interest most, and Cat found that it was a seabed of old-fashioned Mexican tiles, a blue-and-yellow checkerboard that sparkled in the flood of sunlight from above. Here and there some bits of domestic trash had been left behind, and she found herself gliding occasionally over some everyday object made strange by the act of her gliding over it like an airplane sailing just one meter over the floor of the world.

Cat could reach down and touch the floor without diving, and, breathing noisily and rhythmically, getting the hang of the snorkel tube, she started to pick up little things that caught her eye— worthless items like pen caps and one of a dozen old 45 rpm singles that had lost their labels but not their waxy gleam and had settled on the grid of tiles as nicely as new merchandise on a store shelf.

As she hovered over the tiles she began to drift in her mind toward a kind of science fiction story, and finally tried to imagine herself navigating a kind of spacecraft. But that didn't work. Instead she found herself, as she fingered the bits of underwater refuse, remembering only the movie *Pinocchio*, which she had seen years before, and the scenes where Pinocchio and Jiminy Cricket dive heroically into the ocean to search for Geppetto in the belly of the whale. She remembered in strange detail the shimmering, clownish sea world of the cartoon, with its human-faced fish and sea horses, all so unlike the bottom of the laguna. Jiminy had taken a jaunty ride on the back of one of the horses, spurring it on like a jockey, and later, when she and her parents came out of the movie theater in Los Angeles, her father had given her a ride on his shoulders and pretended to be a sea horse pretending to be a thoroughbred, while Penny ran behind and laughed and laughed. How ridiculous, she thought, that the memory of all that would fill her with such a delirious sadness. But she was overcome, and at last had to stand up in the water and gingerly pull the snorkeling mask far enough from her face for the accumulated tears to drain away.

Was it nostalgia? She didn't like to think so. There was no reason to be sentimental, sedimental, no reason to remember her parents as they were. Everyone was still happy, still happy, she told herself. The Inca had his speakers, Penny had her decoupage. And Cat had her submarine. She was her submarine.

Cat stared out across the water in the direction where it reached a couple of miles toward a distant line of mountains. After all, she thought, the water would dry up again, and on the day that it did, she would look back at this day of snorkeling and think, what a stupid way to explore the laguna when she could have just waited for the laguna to disappear. That was the truth about nostalgia—nostalgia was thinking about the past and finally comprehending how much duller and uglier it was than the present.

Cat pinched the mask back on and returned to searching the floor of the drowned house. There would be lots more to find, she thought, but in the end the only thing she swam back with was a rusted camper's hatchet with the red wooden handle still intact.

Back on shore, hunched down behind a line of oleander bushes, shivering and tossing wet hair out of her eyes, she better inspected the little ax. After she rubbed some sand on the steel to get the rust off she thought that it looked almost brand new. She began to daydream.

She imagined that the next day she would go in the car with her father again. After they had ridden awhile, she would quietly bring the little hatchet out and place it in her lap, all without saying a word. Then, in one smooth, unbroken motion, Cat would lunge out with the blade and scrape away the gray bandage, revealing what she was sure must be a pale patch of healthy and unbroken skin underneath the repulsive gauze.

"You lied," she would say, grabbing away her father's microphone and broadcasting her accusations for all to hear. "You told me Mother attacked you but that was something you made up. That's like something out of a romance novel."

Then her daydream became more horrible, more like a nightmare she could not direct or control. Even though she had not meant to imagine such things, for some reason she saw herself attacking her father with the ax, even grabbing The Inca's hair, yanking his head up, and lopping off his head just like the real Incas used to do with copper hatchets. In her dream Cat next ran away guiltily across the desert, ashamed of herself, only to discover that her father's head and then, inexplicably, her mother's head as well, both of them bellowing and cross, were rolling along behind her in pursuit, and that the Mexican desert was no longer Mexico, but had changed into the cold crimson plains of the planet Mars.

"I could make a story out of this," said Cat to herself, bewildered by the sudden advent of her parents into her science fiction plot, but amazed by the vivid colors and swirling details of her imagination.

Except, she thought, the thing is, I'll have to make them into robots, to explain how their heads could roll like that by themselves, and the person running away from the heads will be running like that because she is the only human being left alive on Mars.

Liquid,
Fricative,
Glide

One day Cazden, an administrative assistant, was driving north on Highway C3 and had occasion to pull over just beyond the shadow of the Luxor Avenue bridge. The funny thing was that he had pulled over at just the same spot exactly three years before but, thanks to a chronically poor memory, could not clearly remember why.

Here are the details: The first episode, the one he had trouble remembering, had taken place around two in the afternoon, only hours after Cazden had gone out and bought a new car, a coffee-dark Aplausa with tweed upholstery and climate control. He brought his two-and-a-half-year-old Zoë with him to the dealer's, and from there they inaugurated the new automobile by driving off to Luxorville to a birthday party for three-year-olds. Normally an unruffled and perhaps even under-emotional man, Cazden was surprised to find out how proud of a car, and of himself in one, he could be, even though it was not his dream car, not exactly. The Aplausa was expensive but was not, after all, a Crown Regina like the chancellor drove, and it came with one nagging flaw: a clean bullet hole in the right bottom corner of the windshield which no one at the dealership cared to explain, although the salesman took a hundred dollars off the sticker price after Cazden solemnly pointed it out for the fourth time.

But as he drove and his mind revolved for a moment too much around cars and not enough around his daughter Zoë, less than three years old and more frangible than any new car, he was unaware that, for a moment, everything had gone wrong. A large black insect, gorged with recent feasts of horse or cow blood in the surrounding fields, somehow got sucked in through that same irritating bullet hole in the windshield, and it shot straight through the interior of the car like a second bullet and burst instantly against the inside of the rear windshield, next to where Zoë lay sweetly asleep in her corduroy car seat, and the exploding bug—which Cazden would thereafter refer to as the "horsefly," though he had no way of knowing what it really was—splattered his oblivious baby with twenty or thirty drops of purplish, almost black, animal blood.

The timing of this accident was bad. It was the first weekend Cazden had custody of his daughter since the divorce settlement, and he was nervous about doing well in all his new single-father responsibilities, but he knew himself to be absent-minded, even completely forgetful at times, and he worried about the possibility of forgetting to change Zoë's diaper as promptly as his ex-wife had instructed, or forgetting to feed her lunch, or even forgetting she existed and leaving her behind to suffocate in the car. Let it be said that for the first leg of the trip Cazden fretted far more than was really necessary about the success of the whole outing and checked the rearview mirror every ten seconds or so, adjusting and readjusting it constantly to get an ever-changing, ever-improving view of Zoë, the object of his helpless, clumsy love, as she lay utterly motionless, slack-jawed in baby slumber. But then he did forget about her, if only for a few minutes.

But it doesn't take more than a few minutes, sometimes, for the world to move from love to grief, from serenity to pure hell. Cazden didn't see the bug shoot in through the bullet hole, and for five minutes or more after it had burst softly in the back, he drove on like a bored chauffeur, listing in his mind, as was his habit, some goals he had set himself for the next five years. Here are some of them: better memory skills, more intimacy with his daughter, a better relationship with his boss (a school board trustee), a promotion, a new mom for Zoë. "You don't have to be sick to get better," a motivational tape had once told him, and a minute after the insect's entrance he repeated this remark out loud, a little comforted by the blandness of the bromide, the smoothness of the highway, the ease of piloting a car precisely within the confines of its lane. In fact it was so easy that he started experimenting, weaving a little on the empty highway, and it was some time during those moments spent falling in love with the nimble handling of the new car that he remembered Zoë and lifted a hand to readjust the rearview mirror.

He could not understand or believe what he saw there. Zoë lay sleeping, as before, in her car seat, but her hair and cream-colored party dress were drizzled with something that could not be blood, but could be nothing other than blood.

What should fathers do when they have failed so miserably and betrayed a female trust that only hesitantly, only suspiciously, lets a man—especially a fifty-year-old man—take charge of a toddler for a day? King Midas was a loving father, but he inadvertently turned his daughter's flesh to gold and then staggered away, tearing his robes and begging for divine reprisal. Cazden's impulse was similar. He wanted to scream, to thunder out curses, to drive off the road into a telephone pole and pay penance by ending his life right then. Instead he got a kind of control over himself by whispering again, nonsensically this time, "You don't have to be sick," and carefully pulled off onto a stretch of soft, gravelly shoulder, just past the concrete mass of a bridge that he would learn, three years later, when he had to pull off at that spot again, was called the Luxor Avenue Overpass.

It was cold, but Cazden didn't have a jacket, never needed a jacket in the basin in February, and when he jumped out to open the back door and get to his dead daughter—all the time wondering if she had been shot by a hidden sniper or had simply self-destructed by some method, like crib-death, peculiar to children—a cold wind fluttered his rayon shirt, and the unexpected slap of it shocked him into suddenly believing that no, she was certainly not dead, how could she be dead? And when he finally placed his fingers into the warm, sweet-smelling horse blood on her cheek and heard her somber breathing, and then saw the empty carapace of the horsefly tangled peacefully in her thin blonde hair, he sat down heavily on the edge of the upholstery and wept.

"Wake up, Zoë," he sobbed. "Wake up, baby."

Of course she woke up. Babies always do, and when she did wake up, fluttering her eyes as calmly as King Midas's daughter when he dissolved her golden spell and restored the flesh to life, it started to rain. Cazden had been thinking all day that it probably would rain, the men in the news had all said it was going to, so he was not surprised by the first drops. He felt great that he remembered them saying that it would rain. He plucked his daughter out of the car seat and carried her down the road a few steps, back to where the overpass kept them dry, and it was there, as he cradled and reclaimed his child, that for the first time he came out of himself a little, shook himself out of his vaguenesses and his unfinished lists and his planning, and really looked around him like an artist looking for a landscape. Though what he saw there was not inspiring—it was interesting because it was the first time he had really looked at the bottom side of an overpass with all its stained, dreary concrete and melancholy echoes. He thought to himself, it's like an abandoned church, and then thought that was an idiot's comparison. A few cars sped by with children pressing their faces to back windows to stare at the two of them. One child flashed a peace sign. He sat down on the slope of concrete that angled up sharply toward the bottom of the overshadowing bridge. There he pressed his still sleepy Zoë to him and snuggled his nose into her neck. Then, staring up at the darkest corner of concrete, where there was nothing but a shadowy gap between the top of the slope and the bottom of the bridge, he thought he sensed movement, thought he heard a rustling, thought he could catch something resembling a human and perhaps even tortured kind of sigh.

It all made him a tiny bit nervous, but not scared enough to move away. Then there was no sound, and he thought little more of it.

The rain finally stopped. When the clouds abruptly came apart and the normal monotony of heat and brilliant rural sunshine returned, he held Zoë's hand and they walked back to the car, where he laid her down on the back seat and, for no good reason, changed her diaper. Then he took a moist, perfumed towelette from a plastic box and did his best to wipe the blood off her face and clothes.

"I don't think you can go to a birthday party like that," he said, but he couldn't imagine going back home to Zoë's mother saying that they hadn't gone to the party because a horsefly exploded in the car and the blood ruined the baby's jumper.

No. Better to take her into town, buy her something new to wear, rush her to the party, and then go home with some excuse about the old jumper, how it got chocolate or ink or oil spilled on it and he had had to throw it away.

"Happy birthday to you, happy birthday," sang Zoë as he buckled her back into her car seat.

"Not yet, honey," said Cazden. "Wait until we get to the party and then I want you to sing that song."

But then he stood outside by himself, one hand about to open the driver's door but frozen as he stared into the brown and yellow fields on either side of the road. For some reason it was turning into a day of closer observations. He had never looked so carefully at an underpass before, and now he realized he had never looked closely at the agricultural fields he had driven through a hundred times on the way from Escalera to Luxorville.

What he saw, not far away, on the other side of the highway, sitting in a bath of watery sunlight, was a barn, and on the barn a monumental painted advertisement for a familiar brand of cigarette papers. It was a modern, freshly painted ad, a picture of two giant hands and a pair of smiling lips, even a grotesque tongue slightly protruding to lick the new-made cigarette to a spitty closure. That was it. The fields around the barn were planted with some crop that he did not know the name of but which was ink-green in foliage and beautiful with raspberry-red bouquets. He might have known the name of it once, but of course he was bad at remembering things. That was one way he was not like his father. His father always seemed to know, just by looking at the shape of the leaves or the shade of green, what was planted in any given field, and would announce the names of the crops out loud on Sunday drives, as if to say, you learn this and you remember this because as a farmer you will need to know this. But there were no farmers anymore, only agribusiness executives, and Cazden had ended up an administrator for a school where the students were the children of the agribusiness executives.

As he squinted at the flowers, a crop-dusting helicopter appeared like a fly out of nowhere and roared down on the green and raspberry expanse to breathe out its delicate, rainlike spray.

"That's a dangerous job," he shouted to Zoë as the sweet odor of the fertilizer or pesticide or whatever it was reached his nostrils. "The pilots sometimes crack up, spraying those crops." And then he thought he heard someone say, "Those carrots," and he said to Zoë, after a pause, "Those carrots."

It wasn't until he had gotten back in the car and driven off, and was a few miles down the road, that he realized he had said "Those carrots" without having any idea what he was talking about. And it was strange to realize that he had not said carrots because he had remembered, as he remembered now, that Luxorville had a carrot festival every year, but that he had said it only because he had heard someone else say the word, as if to prompt him with his correct line.

He was sure he had heard a voice, a real, somewhat high-pitched and childish voice that came from a few yards away, from somewhere back near the underpass, from exactly that gap full of shadows where before he thought he had heard a sadness and a hopeless sighing. But then he was not sure he had heard a voice, and it all passed out of memory until the day he heard it, or thought he heard it, again.

Three years later Cazden was still driving the Aplausa. The windshield with the bullet hole had never been replaced, and the tweed seats had been stained over time with ice cream and apple juice and coffee, and the windows were yellowed with a thin film of tobacco tars because Cazden had taken up smoking, and the interior of the Aplausa was the only place he allowed himself this guilty pleasure, smoking there heavily, and often.

What reminded him of the horsefly incident was not the fact that he was driving the same highway to the same little girl's birthday party in Luxorville—he had done that every year, in the same car, on the same route, with Zoë in the same car seat—but the fact that it was starting to rain, in just the feathery, silent way it had rained that day three years before and they had gone for shelter below the overpass. Cazden, still memory-impaired, could not recall that afternoon in any particular detail, but in fact he had a sense that there was something about it he ought to recall but could not. As he drove and watched the slow accumulation of raindrops on the windshield and watched how air pressure flattened each drop into a worm of crystalline water that inched its way to the outer edges of the glass, he could only bring to mind the image of the blood drops that had sprinkled Zoë, the blood that made him gag a little when he first saw it sprayed across her party dress and even spread in a little sheet across the top of her warm blonde hair, like raspberry jam on toast. He felt, in fact, that at the age of fifty-three he was on the verge of losing even the bad memory he had always had. And here is the reward, he told himself, for having a child at so late a juncture in his life that he was unable to bring a younger man's full mental powers to the crucial acts of remembering and knowing and loving a daughter completely.

"Look at the rain, Zoë," he called over his shoulder to where she sat, kitty-corner from him, far across the big interior of the Aplausa, and it was as if talking about the rain, offering the world to her attention, would enrich her life just a little.

"Yes," she sighed, as if other, weightier matters concerned her. Despite the enormous gift that lay next to her on the seat, and despite the special damask ribbon he had helped tie in her hair, and the cartoon character purse (he could never remember the character's name) he had bought for her especially to go with her new party dress, she had seemed moody since he picked her up at her mother's house.

"You know what's funny though, Zoë? I think you'll appreciate the humor of this."

"What?"

"My windshield wipers won't work."

She said nothing, and they drove awhile, both of them listening to the ugly, broken stirrings of the crippled wiper blades and to the rain getting louder and heavier on the roof.

"We're going to have to pull over so I can look at these things, pumpkin. We won't be late to the party. I'm going to pull over under that next bridge."

"Is it a bicycle bridge?"

"Do you mean do bicycles go over it? I guess so. Look, here's a sign. It says, Luxor Avenue. Overpass. OK, people drive cars over it. Can you read a sign like that yet? You know, sweetie, I think we stopped here once before."

It was dark under the concrete, and when Cazden stepped out into the damp wind, a little bit more of that day of three years before came back to him: now he could recall the highway empty of cars, the smell of wet pavement, the gloomy concrete corners and shadows, the barn with its mural (a new ad now, featuring a brilliant white Aplausa), the surrounding fields with their show of rain-darkened green and raspberry-sherbet red. As Cazden plucked lackadaisically at the wiper blades, dimly aware that he had no idea how they functioned, he also recollected his feeling that he and Zoë had not been alone under the overpass, that all the while—at least this is how he remembered it—someone had been watching them, and especially judging him, Cazden, as he held his daughter, wiped the blood off her face, watched the sun come out, drove on.

Back in the driver's seat, he lazily, absentmindedly, lit a cigarette. It was fairly apparent to him now that there never had been anyone there, and he thought he could explain, or start to explain, why he had imagined someone being there.

"Daddy, you know you're not supposed to smoke when I'm with you."

Cazden glanced in the rearview mirror, and there was his daughter, frowning, maybe even on the verge of angry tears, and he guiltily, forcefully, tossed the cigarette out the window and watched it roll, still glowing, into the road, where it finally blinked out in the rain.

"Zoë, remember the day that bug got in the car, a few years ago, and you got a little blood on your dress? Remember that?"

"Daddy, you know what? I've been meaning to tell you something about that. You told me that was a horsefly. But you're wrong. I read in my insect book that horseflies don't live in California. It must have been something else."

"Well OK, Miss Smart Aleck, then what was it?"

"I don't know."

"Then it was a horsefly."

"And you also told me that day that these were carrot fields. But they're not. That crop with all the raspberry flowers is alfalfa. And they shouldn't grow alfalfa here because it uses up so much water and only cows eat it."

He thought then that as soon as the rain stopped he would get Zoë to her birthday party. But not stay. He couldn't stand her to talk that way to him, as she often did now, and he didn't want to be surrounded by kids all day, not if they were getting to the age where they could tell you things you ought to know but don't.

In fact he had a little plan all his own. If there was enough time, like three or four hours, before having to retrieve Zoë, he thought he would drop by the house of an interesting woman named Luisa, whose address he had already looked up in the phone book and written down. At a planning meeting the week before they had met and talked. She was new to the school district and he thought he had detected an interest on her part, an unspoken hint, evident to him in her smile, the tilt of her head, that she would like to talk again sometime, perhaps the sooner the better. His idea was that he would buy a nice bouquet of flowers and just show up on her front porch, without phoning first or anything, barging into her life with a spontaneity and winsomeness that would prove, perhaps, irresistible.

Half an hour later, with the sky full of sunlight and low-flying airliners from the nearby airport and a bright rainbow arching like candy over the chimney of the birthday house, Cazden and Zoë threaded their way through a line of parked cars to the backyard, and father watched with satisfaction as daughter fled into the melee of six-year-olds. Then, standing near the refreshment table, where the parents of the birthday girl had put out bottles of Chardonnay on ice for the adults, Cazden looked around and was astonished to find himself face to face with a six-year-old that was as tall as he was, a little girl much like Zoë staring at him eye to eye and frowning like she was about to cry. Then it was clear—and he had to laugh at his stupid, split-second misperception—that the giant was in fact a normal child clutched by her mother in such a way as to meld the child's face onto the mother's body, and suddenly the little girl was detached, was on the ground, running and screaming toward her playmates, and the mother was straightening up and smiling at him.

"I'm Zoë's dad," he smiled, but she frowned and looked away as she spoke.

"I don't know these kids," she said. "I hardly know anybody here."

It wasn't until then that he realized that this was the woman he had chatted with at the planning meeting—the woman he had wanted to call.

"Of course I know you," he smirked, covering his error, wondering if she knew he hadn't recognized her. "And your name is—" But horribly, typically, he had now forgotten her name.

"Luisa Beckmann," she smiled, offering a hand to shake while draining a plastic tumbler of Chardonnay with the other.

She was about fifty but looked forty-five, with abundant ice-white hair, a slim choreographer's body, and a ceremonious, bureaucratically formal cast to her attire. While other women near the refreshment table or seen hopping on the lawn with the children were dressed in jeans and sweats, Luisa was rather exquisite in heels, tweedy skirt, and a silk scarf printed with Roman or Byzantine mosaics and picturesquely draped low over her shoulders.

"I knew you lived in Luxorville," cried Cazden, trying to rescue himself, trying to animate his features and his voice in a way that he hoped she might sense as charming, "but I never thought Luxorville was so small that I would find you at a random party."

He knew at once that sounded bad—random party!—but she laughed, he thought, like a girl falling in love. Maybe it was a drunken laugh, but that was all right. Then, because she said nothing, just slowly tossed M & M's one at a time onto her lethargic tongue, expressionless behind a pair of enormous hexagonal sunglasses, he went on.

"That was your daughter? What a cutie pie. I can see that there are—I can see that you have a lot of good chromosomes in your family."

"I'm sorry," she finally said, swallowing. "I know we've met but I just can't come up with your name."

"Oh, it's Cazden, Cazden. Remember? Lou Cazden. Board of trustees." He felt that, in order to seem less eager, he should not appear to know her name so well, but forgot that he had already had the initial moment of forgetting it. He repeated, "Luisa. Lou and Luisa. Your name's Luisa, isn't that right?"

She raised her fist near her face again, this time without candy, but it was another long time, a painfully long time, before she spoke.

"Luisa Beckmann." This time without a smile.

Then Cazden, half out of a frantic awkwardness and half out of an abstracted aspiration to give her a sample of who he was and what was important to him, launched unexpectedly into the story of the overpass.

It was a long story. After all, it had two parts: the episode of the horsefly and its blood, which he remembered pretty well now, and the episode of ending up back in that same spot years later and remembering that he couldn't remember everything.

"And," he concluded, as she reached for the wine bottle again and refilled both their glasses with a gurgle of the greenish transparent wine, "I think I know why I felt we were being watched both times. I remembered as I was parking the Aplausa—"

He stopped, confused for a moment where he was in the story.

"I drive an Aplausa," he blurted, foolishly, "though my dream car is one of those Crown Reginas, like the chancellor drives."

But Luisa, preoccupied with a rapid series of odd tiny sips of wine, all in the manner of someone who is afraid of spilling an overfilled glass, did not seem to hear this part, and he recovered and went on with the story.

"At any rate I know I saw an article and some photographs in the newspaper about this. About homeless people, I mean, or hobos, or immigrants—maybe it was all three—who live under freeways. You know, there's a kind of space, an overhang place under the overpass, where some of these people have set up all their belongings."

"I read," said Luisa, swallowing, "I read just recently about a man who saved all the shoes he ever wore in his life."

Cazden couldn't see the connection to his story, but he was charmed by her heavy drinking, as well as gallant enough to concede the conversational turn to her.

"It was an old man in Egypt, I think, and it was terrible. I mean, it wasn't like Imelda Marcos, or anything like that, for the man was terribly poor. Well, he couldn't have been that poor if he'd had so many shoes, could he? At any rate, he had kept all his shoes, beginning with his little white baby boots, and placed them all on the floor against the walls of his living room, so you would walk around the perimeter of the room, and see, through the shoes, his evolution into an old man. The magazine was making it into a kind of joke, but I thought it was the saddest story I ever heard."

"Why? I mean, I don't see what makes it so sad."

"I haven't finished the story," she said in a somewhat harassed tone, as if she expected Cazden to have known it couldn't be over. She adjusted her scarf in such a way as to unveil, for a moment, a hint of cleavage and a drift of old-fashioned, florid perfume. "See, someone ended up stealing all his shoes. Out of his house. And why on earth were they stolen? The most recent pair was as shabby and down in the heels as the first. But I expect the truly poor were given the shoes. None of us should hoard what we have, Mr. Cazden, or make fun of those who have nothing."

"That reminds me of a story," said Cazden.

"Which one?"

Cazden took a bold step forward, knowingly invading the space they had negotiated between their two somewhat stiff, somewhat self-conscious bodies.

"The story I just told you, about the guy who lives under the overpass. Underpass."

"Oh that," she giggled, waving her hand extravagantly within the few inches of space that separated them. "Excuse my French, but that story seemed kind of, um, like bullshit? People do not live under freeways like that, not out here. That's something that would go on in L.A. Not on Highway C3. What would they eat? Where would they go to get work?"

Cazden was sure she was drunk now, or at least farther along in her drinking than he was, but that didn't prevent him feeling a little alarmed at the notes of anger and perplexity he thought he heard in her voice.

"What do you know about poor people anyway?" she asked, smiling.

"Well, do you at least believe the part about the horsefly?" he asked.

But that question did not seem to register.

"Were you ever homeless, Mr. Cazden? Did you ever have to live like that, like those poor souls under the freeway? You see, I did, once. Not under a freeway, I mean, but I had it pretty tough, like those guys, and I can guarantee you that there are no people living out there on the highway. I can guarantee you that."

"Wanna bet?" he countered, childlike, thinking that now they had really reached the deluxe bullshitting. He was sure she was lying about being poor once, and then, suddenly, not so sure, wondering if she might not be originally from Mexico. Her name was Luisa, after all, and although she was clearly well-heeled, successful now, a self-assured professional woman in her heels and scarf and Chardonnay, he thought she just might be a Mexican, and he now could picture her, as he pictured Mexicans, mired in poverty as a child, roaming around the dusty streets of some squalid village, face marred by patches of ringworm, scabies, impetigo, all the childhood blemishes which he had read about in his infant-care books and which he often imagined he could see coming into bloom on his daughter's skin. As he ran these images through his head he felt at once embarrassed and yet somehow victorious. Here was an inspiration: that the key to seducing her, to making her love him, to turning her into Zoë's new mom, would be in knowing her past and demonstrating to her in one stroke how utterly in tune to and how favorable he was to poverty, to Mexicanness, to the celebration of self-motivation and influence over others, to the celebration of being what? Well, not a Loser anyway, not a Mexican, but an Achiever.

"Let's go see," she sneered at him before he could say it himself, taking hold of his upper arm rather heavily, rather unsteadily. "Let's drive out to your overpass and see who's there. The kids'll be all right. We'll be back a long time before the party's over."

Her car, it turned out, was a Crown Regina, like the chancellor's, and when they came up to it Cazden swallowed, and shrank—then roused himself enough to admire its deep purple-gray color and windows as tinted and murky as Luisa's sunglasses. The velvet seats were fragrant and dark, as in a Victorian drawing room, the door closed with a clean industrial clunk, and when Luisa turned the key in the ignition a strange tiny female voice said, "The external temperature is now eighty-nine degrees." But then she turned the key back the other way, killing all the little lights and voices that had sprung up, and she froze where she sat, with her thin but loosely fleshed arms hung over the steering wheel like velvet draperies.

"Can we take your car?" she whispered. "Can you drive, hon? I guess I'm not feeling all that great." It was strange, but it seemed to him that she acted more and more drunk, without drinking anything. "Can *you* please drive, Mr. Cazden?" There was a hint of helpless pleading in her voice which he did not like, and what's more he hated her to see how old and dirty and full of debris his car was. But then she got out and came around to his side of the car, and he realized that she meant he should drive her car.

On the way back to the overpass, he dozed off for a fraction of a second. His head snapped down, then up. He gripped the steering wheel like a man gripping the bars of his jail cell, breathed in the thick chrysanthemum smell of his passenger's perfume, and suddenly felt more awake than he had felt all day.

"My God," he said aloud, forgetting that Luisa was next to him in the passenger seat. "That time I could have killed myself."

"That won't be necessary," she sighed, and he gave another little start to hear her voice so close to his ear. "If you lose our bet, you won't have to kill yourself. What was it you promised if there's no one under the overpass? What was it you said you would buy me?"

"A drink?" He had no recollection of any promises.

"No," she moaned in her low, textured voice—a voice in which he strained now, without success, to hear some trace of a Mexican accent. "It was better than that. I think you said you were going to get me a new scarf. It was when you were talking so much about my scarf, remember?"

But he couldn't remember. All he could think of now was of making love to her, and he didn't want to hear her voice anymore, just wanted to drive and drive with perfect concentration and speed and get the two of them to the overpass as soon as possible.

One problem was that he could not remember the name of the overpass. Would he recognize it? Would he be able to find the right one? He thought he had better not think about that, and focused himself instead on what he planned to do once he got them there. His concept of the hobo's hideout, the tucked away shelter in the crook of the overpass, had changed, and now instead of seeing it as the residence of his enemy, the filthy but sardonic being who had sat up there and watched him and laughed at him on the two occasions he had had over the years to park there, he now saw it as something more like a buddy's empty apartment, a trysting place, a secret love nook. The only difference was in who would be there, really. The tramp, the illegal alien, or whatever he was, would be gone, and, just like in the photographs Cazden had seen in the newspaper, they would find flattened cardboard boxes for a floor, shopping carts full of castoff groceries, pesticide buckets turned into sinks, even a coffee table fashioned out of produce crates. Most of all there would be a mattress on the floor, a little grungy but not impossibly foul, and there he and Luisa—Luisa who said herself she had once lived that life and so must know how to accommodate to such conditions—would sink down into an hour of exquisite and gritty love-making. There he would help her to remove her scarf, her dress, her old-fashioned lacy lingerie. Then, as strong and red as a horse, he would move into her without hesitation or tiring or forgetfulness, doing his work until she sang out greedily for greater action, greater focus, wrapped a leg around him in such a way that one ankle bone would dig in just below his buttocks and guide him a little farther along, down to the spot where both their greeds could finally burst, then fade into exhaustion.

But there, in the air-conditioned Crown Regina, she seemed simply bored, and stared out her window in such a perfunctory, nonconversational way that the only positive thing he could see in their relationship thus far was that she had not seemed to notice how carefully he scrutinized every underpass they glided under.

"So—what's your favorite thing about being a trustee?" she asked—sighed, really—and he could feel that in asking it she was reaching to the very bottom of her small-talk repertoire. Wasn't there something almost tortured in her sigh?

"I'm sorry, Luisa," he said, "but I wouldn't want you to go away with the impression that I'm a trustee. Trustees here are elected officials. You must know that. I'm Sandra Fujiwara's assistant. I'm an assistant to a trustee.

"Now what about you," he went on after a long pause. "You must tell me what you do besides raise that wonderful daughter of yours."

"Well, you know, I'm a speech pathologist for the district. You know: the lady who comes around once a year to see what sounds the kids are having problems with? I profile their speech problems. Liquids, fricatives, glides. All that. Stuttering is bad in this district. You wouldn't think that stuttering would be more common one place than another, would you? But this district is where you get the stutterers. Maybe as trustee or trustee's assistant, or whatever you are, you know all this already."

"I don't know anything. Those words you said. I could never remember words like that. What's a fricative? It sounds like a way to cook chicken. Chicken fricative."

But she didn't get the joke, or at least didn't laugh or sidle closer to him on the seat. Didn't drape her arm around his neck or nibble at his earlobe, nor did he begin to drive with a jaunty, possessive smile. Luisa just turned back to staring out the window at the fields and said nothing, was so moribund and unfriendly that when the Luxor Avenue Overpass finally came into view and he concluded, in a triumph of memory, that this was the one he was afraid he would forget, and did not forget, he pulled over without comment. The fields were colored green and raspberry, and he remembered, with a nod of his head, that Zoë had identified that crop. She taught him that it was alfalfa.

They crossed the highway on foot and stood in the exact spot where he had stopped with Zoë twice before. The difference was that now it was nearly dusk and the low sun lit up the underpass with an incredible orange light, and as they trudged up the concrete it was like climbing the slope of some fiery volcano.

"We've got to get this over with," cried Luisa, halfway up, her voice echoing strangely, as if in a bunker. "The party will be over and the kids will be waiting for us."

Cazden could only think, she's right, and still make no effort to undo his fantasy.

As they got near the top they could still see well. There was no darkness, no mystery, and when their heads finally came up short against the bottom of Luxor Avenue and they could climb no farther, it was evident that there was nothing to see there. The orange light had turned a little purple. Cazden wanted to point out how in fact the slope leveled off enough at the top that someone could live there if they wanted to, if they could stand living in a five-foot-high space. Then he noticed a flattened-out cardboard box and thought to himself, that could be someone's bed, or tablecloth.

He thought, maybe someone does live here in this concrete bunker. Well, he thought, it's ambiguous.

It might be said that a lousy memory doesn't matter, because things everywhere are a little ambiguous. Cazden stooped to sit down painfully on the dusty cardboard, and there he relaxed and gathered in the unforgettable smell of cement, not trying to remember anything anymore, and when at last he noticed that Luisa was already stumbling down the purple slope, already getting back in her car, already starting the engine and leaning long and bitterly on the horn, he couldn't imagine what her hurry was.

Miss
Mustachioed
Bat

Almost all the tentative intimacy of their friendship ended when Claudette tried to frighten phobic Tina by tossing the damp bandeau top of her bikini toward her and shouting, insipidly, "Watch out for that mustachioed bat!"

Tina dodged, and the bandeau top slapped harmlessly on the cement. Then she dove neatly into the pool and refused to come up for air.

Claudette was sorry. Tiptoeing to the edge of the pool, she knew she had been stupid. At the same time there was no doubt in her mind that Tina was hamming things up too much by making herself invisible at the very bottom of the pool and pretending to have drowned.

There was a sunset of golden light right then, there was no fence to their backyard, and Claudette kept moving her glance back and forth from the still water to a single electrical tower, unwired, that glowed there against the mountain like a spire in Oz.

Claudette and Tina had liked each other from their first meeting and had never expected anything like this to happen. They were certain to remain friends.

Both began working at India Basin College at the same time, in the year of the whitefly infestation, when the crop dusters carried on so long in the fields around the campus that every breeze carried a sharp, brassy flavor of insecticide. Claudette was an instructor in the Developmental Communications Department and Tina had a job as an administrator in Special Services. They met at a breakfast for retiring faculty, where, perhaps because they were the two youngest people in the hall, they gravitated to the same table. Claudette was twenty-nine, tall with rounded, broad-boned shoulders and a braided, yard-long ponytail that hung down her spine like a whip, while Tina was short-haired, polished, precise, a year younger than Claudette, full of fingertip nervousness and adjustments of her oversize glasses. They paid scant attention to each other at first, only exchanging a couple of curious glances and smiles. Then when one of the retirees, a certain Doctor LeBaron from Speech and Broadcasting, advanced to the lectern to receive his gifts from the dean, Claudette turned to Tina and said loudly enough for everyone at the table to hear, "So why didn't we give him something when he retired five years ago?"

Tina was puzzled, flustered to be singled out. "I thought he was just retiring now," she laughed.

"I mean," smirked Claudette, "when he retired from rational thought."

Tina could not keep down a slightly scandalized laugh. Claudette peered at her table partner with an arched eyebrow, admiring the way Tina laughed with a pursed-lip, whistling sound, and added, less cleverly, this time turning away from Tina, "A nice little basket-weaving kit would have been appropriate."

Tina laughed and whistled again, and from then on, whenever they ran into each other on campus, they chatted or, better, Claudette joked and Tina ran out of breath with laughing at it all and closed her eyes and adjusted her glasses, and sometimes felt altogether a little slow, a little small.

Then they decided to become roommates. Claudette coincidentally broke up with a boyfriend in the same week that Tina was evicted from her apartment and together they found a just-constructed house for rent on the edge of the newest tract.

Then they began to discover that their personalities were not always complementary. Claudette was native to the basin and had in her some of its slow-motion cynicism, its resignation to a cozy and perpetual unimportance. Tina, transplanted there from the big city, was upbeat, anxious to love small-town life, and endearingly straight. It was a noticeable trait of Tina's that, in the midst of some repartee, she would not so much miss as ignore many of Claudette's exquisite put-downs. Even while she perfectly understood the edge of some intended exaggeration or even dishonesty in Claudette's tone, she would charge back with a cheery, heartfelt humanism that left Claudette laughing at her and left Tina feeling more and more sanguine about their friendship. As a result Claudette found herself slowly retreating toward a broader, coarser humor, not understanding why, and finally, a month after they met, in the unfinished yard of their new house, Tina, stung by the idea of the wet bandeau top, dove in grief to the bottom of the pool and swam and swam through dark water and chlorine, unable to see the cement bottom but scratching her stomach against it as she willed herself from bubbling back to the surface.

She was not a good swimmer. But it occurred to her that it was wrong to think that she had to keep moving to stay submerged, and she hooked a finger through a hole in the drain at the bottom of the deep end and fixed herself there, elegantly upside down, like a delicate plastic mermaid in an aquarium. There, cheeks puffed up with carbon dioxide, she could focus all her concentration on that part of the brain that one has constantly to persuade, when holding one's breath, not to surrender. Oh don't breathe, she said to her lungs, don't you dare take a breath. Don't give up this moment of miniature pride.

Above her, tiptoeing around the edge of the pool, Claudette fretted, feeling her own grief, her own stupidity, and she started breathing raggedly, biting her bitten-down nails, trying to see where Tina—normally the sissy, normally afraid to swim underwater because in fact she couldn't hold her breath for more than a few seconds—had disappeared to. But it was already starting to get a little dark in the valley. It didn't occur to Claudette to flip on the underwater lights, and she couldn't see anything in the pool except, at the surface, a tiny fractured reflection of sunset gold.

There was a breeze out of the south that ran across her skin like hot water.

"Oh please stop it right now, all this silliness," she finally shrieked at the pool, bending her knees and cupping her hands around her mouth, like a swimming coach. "Get your butt out of there, Tiny. You know I was just kidding you the way I always do." Then shouting again with flustered emphasis, but unable to resist an extra twist, she added, "That really wasn't a bat."

But nothing. Just the surface of the water, serene as melted gold.

Then Claudette got really scared, and then so mad at herself for being scared, for being taken in by Tina's dumb performance, that she was close to diving in, head first, if only to complete the sense of the theatrical with a performance that in fact would require some daring. But five seconds passed, and then five more, and she still couldn't make the decision to enter Tina's world.

Meanwhile, below water, Tina had held her breath longer than ever before in her life. She knew that it felt like, but probably wasn't, sixty seconds. She had read about yogis who could hold it much longer, but for her of course there would be brain damage. Finally the clenching of the lungs became too painful, and she knew she had to give up the anger, and go back home to the air.

Only to find that her finger, in the drain, was stuck. She gave it a bone-stretching yank, and realized that she was just more stuck than before, that her finger was perhaps swelling up somehow in the dense water at the bottom of the pool. A terrible pain bloomed and grew in the pulmonary sacs like black flowers, filling her whole chest with doom, and her last thought, at the moment that she finally, almost unconsciously reached with her other hand to twist the drain and so finally free the finger and begin to buoy up slowly, horrifically slowly, through bright water toward the surface of the pool, was that even then she was not going to make it, that drowning was not what she had always imagined, a sad and passive way to die, but a violent murder, a tearing apart by water and fire.

Then Tina's head broke through, near the deep end of the pool.

And all the evening air she wanted, with its gift of great warm volumes of oxygen, even though laced with pesticides, was there, and the hollow in her chest turned sunny and cheerful and optimistic. She always felt afterward that she really had died about halfway on her journey up, but that the small-town sky had forced itself down her dead throat like the breath of some wonderful small-town lifeguard.

Finally, when at last she got her senses back, she realized that her roommate was nowhere in sight.

It was funny but perhaps not surprising that all Tina's fine dignity and drama had evaporated by then, or maybe spent itself in that second when she died. Yet, on finding that Claudette had abandoned her, she had to go back and look for the anger she had lost and put it on again, like a lost wrap. "Claudette," she said aloud, convincing herself more thoroughly that way, "is despicable."

But as soon as she succeeded in this way in getting angry again, she lost it, and remembered that one of her many confused thoughts during the moments of true drowning was a wish for her roommate to appear out of nowhere, grab her in her arms, and play the part of the small-town lifeguard.

Meanwhile, Claudette still didn't appear, still didn't come galloping out of the house with a first aid kit, or an oxygen tank, and what was Tina to do with a friend like that? She imagined with a fresh shudder of fury that her roommate must have casually, drunkenly ambled back into the house, leaving a fellow human being to drown at the bottom of the pool, as if that were the way backyard barbecues were expected to end.

Then she felt some movement under the water. Something brushed, porpoiselike, against her toes, even cupped the toes for a moment in its hand, and she fathomed with a gasp of laughter and renewed affection that it was Claudette, swimming underwater, looking for her, finally aware that she was too late to save any lives. Tina stayed quiet and a moment later, at the far, shallow end of the pool, Claudette emerged, dripping and sluggish, still wearing only her cut-off jeans, now waterlogged, which she kicked off with difficulty before marching silently, nakedly, into the house. Once inside she threw on so many lights and audibly slammed so many doors that Tina, still breathing in the corner of the pool, unseen and unsought, hardly knew what to think, couldn't imagine if Claudette was infuriated with her, or disoriented, or just exhausted from her underwater reconnaissance.

It was deep twilight by then. The air was marbled with cool and warm patches and Tina could glimpse a string of stars—could it be some astral somebody's belt?—above the summit of the hill. Claudette did not come back out into the yard but kept turning on lights until it looked like the house was on fire. Tina stayed in the pool and thought about a more pleasant time, a walk with Claudette on campus the week before, when Claudette said something about the president of the college she couldn't even remember now but that made her laugh and whistle so hard she had to stop and lean against the wire fence around the tennis courts. "Oh Claudette," she remembered saying, hardly able to speak through her giggles and tears, "you say the cruelest things about people. The cruelest, most wonderful things."

They had spent the whole of that long Sunday afternoon lounging in the unfinished yard, inaugurating things. Claudette called it an "official bourgeois barbecue, and with hot dogs because they go so well with the mustard flavor of the insecticides."

The day before, they had driven to the mall in town and spent a little on two wire lawn chairs and a strange domed barbecue with handles placed in such a way that it looked like a samurai's helmet, and they arranged these three items on the narrow margin of cement around the pool, their only patio.

On this cement in fact they were symbolically and half-physically confined, because to step off the patio was to step into a scratchy and uninviting wilderness. There was really no backyard, or, rather, the desert was their backyard. No fence had ever been put up, and their house stood on the very edge of the subdivision. A few feet from the edge of the pool grew a clump of twisted, faintly fragrant sage, the first of thousands that spread from there far up the slope of an endless hill, together with thistles and gray-green stickseed. Farther out, the electrical tower grew out of a sickly patch of yellow soil. As they barbecued chicken breasts and chicken franks, they thrust their faces into smoke and heat every few minutes to paint the meat with a thin solution of tomato, vinegar, and herbs. Later, after they had eaten it all up in great mouthfuls, crooning their satisfaction, and left the bones to dry in the evening heat on paper plates, they sat drinking white wine from cups from the bathroom dispenser and listening to the call of a bird that they both had to admit they did not know the name of.

"I'm not as happy with that mountain—or that tower—as I thought I'd be," said Claudette, slumped so far down in her wire chair that her navel had disappeared into a deep crevasse across her stomach.

Tina, sitting cross-legged on her chair, as if on a stool, was surprised. "Oh no," she protested. "To think that I was just about to say how beautiful it is. I love the outline it makes against the sky, the mountain I mean, with those boulders at the top. I don't know. Maybe it's not as nice as it could be."

"You like it? I think it looks like an upside-down ice cream cone, without the ice cream. You know? See how that shoulder sticks out? And how it's flat on top, even with the boulders? Let's call it Mount Saf-T-Kon, shall we? For me it would be so much nicer with some cactus."

"I like cactus," sighed Tina. "When I applied to the college, the job description said something about desert landscape, and immediately I pictured cactus, something like in *Krazy Kat*. But I guess I should have been imagining something more like the Sahara, more like that other cartoon, what's it called, about the foreign legion? But I do like that mountain."

"Not me. Not Mount Saf-T-Kon."

"It's just that you've lived here too long," Tina observed. "You don't know how to like the landscape anymore."

"What I need is a car that runs well enough to get me out of here sometimes," said Claudette, sinking lower in her chair.

"No, you need to get out on hikes. You know, a group from Special Services is planning a hike around the north end of the reservoir next weekend. Why don't we go and, I know, we'll take a notebook and start a list of things. We'll start a journal for identifying birds and plants and stuff."

"How could we know their names?"

"We'll buy a book. An identification guide."

"That sounds like a lot of fun," Claudette cracked, straightening up and smiling and nodding. But this was one of those times that Tina caught the sarcasm.

"Oh, you're evil," Tina exclaimed, standing up to pour more wine. "I think this wine tastes like pineapple juice."

"Hey, you have a grid pattern on your thighs," commented Claudette. "Just like the franks."

Tina ran her fingers along the pattern the chair had left on her skin and let out a snort. "And it's so hot I feel barbecued," she brayed.

"It's not that hot," Claudette remarked, coolly. "I've never seen you this drunk, have I?"

Tina stopped laughing, folded a towel to fit on the chair, and sat down with her feet flat on the ground, without having poured herself another glass.

"No one has seen me this drunk because I have never been this drunk," she said softly.

"Hmm," said Claudette. "Let's talk about who we're going to invite for our first party."

"Chez nous? But I like to talk about being drunk."

"Talking about drinking will keep you from drinking."

"Let's invite everybody we know."

"You're still not drinking your pineapple juice. You have some more, Tina, and I'll tell you what I know about the bats around here."

"Oh please."

"No, no, I don't mean tell you to scare you. I mean talk about them rationally. You, Miss Bat, are the one who suggested it."

Tina wasn't sure. It was true that they had recently agreed they should take time to explore and perhaps undo her chiropterphobia, her fear of bats. Tina wanted to get over it. She had explained to her roommate how she started using the more scientific term, chiropterphobia, in order to achieve greater objectivity. Claudette admired this rationalism and admitted to some phobias of her own (getting her hands dirty, sitting on public toilet seats). Both acknowledged that such fears were irrational but were also quite real to the sufferer and were worthy of some measure of dignity, some respect. Besides, Tina had explained, her problem with bats was not nearly as bad as it had been in childhood—when she had once screamed and thrown a *National Geographic* across the room because of a close-up photo of a bat's shocking, intestinelike face—and there was every chance she might get over it someday if people would leave her alone and, as she now recalled having said to Claudette, "If you would help me with it in a civilized and supportive way."

"Now, what was it," asked Tina, glancing warily at Claudette, putting her fingers to her cheeks, adjusting her glasses, "that you wanted to say about them?"

"First, how sorry I feel that, while we sit here enjoying our cactusless backyard, you have to worry a little bit about one coming along and spoiling everything."

"I wasn't thinking about them at all."

"Well," sighed Claudette, as if reluctant to say what she had to say, "maybe you should think, because I have to tell you that I saw one just a minute ago."

"Oh. You did? That's interesting. Where?" Tina measured out her reaction calmly, as if she were writing an essay, but at the same time she placed one foot in front of the other in a subconscious preparation to start walking far away.

"At least I thought I saw one, Tiny. It was way up there, flitting around those rocks. Gone now. Isn't the sunset nice? I just think that they do tend to come out around this time of evening."

"Well, Claudette, I very much appreciate your telling me this. I—" Tina stopped speaking, then giggled. "I guess it can't hurt to have a kind of scientific discussion about them, can it?" Meanwhile a sort of milky, lacy sensation, the poison of the phobia, had spread across the skin on her neck, her chest, her stomach. She knew from awful experience that this tingling was likely to turn soon into an angry, splotchy rash.

"Oh, if it's science you want, that's what I'm good at."

"You're not serious."

"I am serious."

"You didn't know the name of that bird."

"An ornithologist I'm not."

"What's the name of this plant?" asked Tina, kicking the nearest bush with her toe. Now all her skin was on fire.

"Sage, Tiny. But I wonder—is it recipe sage, the kind you cook with? Or is it Riders of the Purple Sage? Or are they the same thing?"

Tina sat up straight in her chair, tugged the bottom edge of her swimsuit down, tried to secretly exorcise her fear a little by rubbing her legs, trying not to scan the horizon. Somehow it helped to change her posture again, to bring her knees up to her chin and wrap herself up into a kind of ball, or fortress.

Claudette continued. "So, to go on, I was telling you about how they do, uh, come out at this hour. They live in caves in the mountains, you know, mountains like Mount Saf-T-Kon, but across the border. They're called leaf-nosed bats, because their noses are deformed in a bizarre way. They literally resemble leaves, Tina, let's say sage leaves, fresh sage. What the purpose of this leaf shape may be, I can't tell you. I mean my research didn't carry me that far. But there's more, I can almost quote the book: bats in general are a friend and benefactor to mankind because of their habit of devouring untold millions of enemy insects every night. Also, hmm, they pollinate bananas and avocados. They pose no threat to humans and in fact strenuously avoid humans, under all circumstances, with— Well, with one or two exceptions. You know you wanted me to tell you all this."

Staring into the swimming pool, Tina imagined herself attacked by thousands of bats at once in such a way that they covered every inch of her skin like bees on a beekeeper, and though they couldn't sting her, somehow they nibbled her away, drained her. That was half her daydreaming. The other half consisted of bits of a cartoon she had seen once as a child. But why this cartoon? It had a sewing machine that went out of control and careened around the landscape, madly sewing up everything in sight that was somehow torn or open, beginning with holes in trees, then gaping bystanders' mouths, then going on to stitch up a swimming pool, a football stadium, and finally the Atlantic and the Pacific oceans, sewing the whole planet in such a way that it looked like a lumpy baseball, with too-tight continents stretched painfully around the globe.

"I'm thinking about a sewing machine right now," she said, still staring into the water, still also thinking of the beehive bats, "and I'm not sure why."

"Hmm."

"So what are the exceptions?"

"Exceptions?"

"The two exceptions you said where bats will attack humans."

"Tiny, I never said they would attack humans. I meant that there's one situation where they won't go out of their way to avoid you, and that is, around a body of water. I hate to tell you this. If you're getting too nervous, let me know and I'll shut up. But I understand that bats love lakes and ponds and yes even swimming pools. Because they love to skim over the water hunting insects, and that's exactly where zoologists go when they want to get a chance to see them."

Claudette stood up out of her chair, then took a step forward, revealing how the backs of her bare legs, just under the ragged hem of her cut-offs, had also been stamped with a crimson waffle pattern by the chair. Then, as if convinced by her own words to go off and meet the bats face to face, she jumped feet first, like a ten-year-old, into the pool, splashing some drops of water into the barbecue, where they hissed like snakes.

That left Tina alone. And, for a little while longer, that was all right. She could go in the house anytime she wanted to. She understood perfectly that there was nothing to be afraid of. After all, she had dissected mice in high school, pinning the creatures down to the dissecting board without a twinge of disgust, coolly slicing their ventral cavities for a close look at the spongy pancreas, the cunningly designed little heart, and she knew that bats were mice, or very nearly so, with wings stretched out from fingertip to tip of tail and endowed, it was always, always pointed out, with extraordinary powers of hearing and navigation.

"I forgot to mention something interesting." It was Claudette, back from her lap across the pool, leaning on the edge of the shallow end, almost whispering, serious, looking around as if she were about to reveal a secret. "They call 'em mustachioed bats."

"What are?"

"The bats I was telling you about. This particular species is called the mustachioed bat, because the leaf-shaped nose also looks a little like a mustache."

Tina slid forward on her chair and lowered her face toward the heat that still floated up like gas from the last red embers of the barbecue and held the towel behind her head in such a way as to trap and concentrate the heat even more.

"This is a bat I guess I have to see," she said to the fire, but speaking loud enough for Claudette to hear.

"So you like the idea?" Claudette was excited for a moment. "You amaze me. You've come around."

"So they make them with mustaches now, do they?"

"Like I told you," Claudette said cheerily, and lazily dipped and redipped her arms in the water.

"And do these particular bats live around here?" asked Tina.

"You weren't listening before, Miss Mustachioed Bat," responded Claudette. "I mentioned that they do come up occasionally from Mexico, from Mexican caves."

"That seems appropriate."

"What?"

"That mustachioed bats come from Mexico. Doesn't the president of Mexico have a mustache?"

"Everyone in Mexico," said Claudette, "has a mustache. Even the women."

Tina drew away from the fire and reared her head, in time to see that Claudette was hoisting herself up the stainless steel ladder and out of the pool. She watched quietly as Claudette stripped off her cut-off jeans, rubbed herself hastily with a towel, twisted the excess water out of the jeans, and jerked them back on.

"What a perfectly ridiculous and bigoted statement," Tina said, standing up and walking close to Claudette. It was the first time she had ever gone against her. But Claudette flashed a clownish, spastic smile, collapsed in her wire chair, and fumbled for the wine.

Tina walked away a few steps. She had forgotten for the moment about her fear. When she stumbled a little, she decided she was getting too drunk to walk tightrope-style around the pool and turned back toward Claudette. Just then she heard her roommate's voice shout, "Watch out for that mustachioed bat!" and something black and sinister came flapping noiselessly toward her.

––––––––––

For a long time after the near drowning, after Claudette went inside and turned on all the lights in the house, Tina stayed in the water. She liked the darkness and wetness and had mostly forgotten about bats, especially real bats. A gust of wind came around the base of Mount Saf-T-Kon, smelling of sagebrush and neighbors' barbecues, and Tina felt strength come back with it, together with a kind of wisdom that said, all right, find Claudette. Find her and forgive her. Forgive because it is wise to forgive, and because, in fact, between that brief, brief moment when she saw something black flying toward her face and wondered if it had real possibilities of batness, and the moment when that something missed her, and she noticed Claudette's bare breasts and tentative expression, and found herself trying to pick up Claudette's bandeau top with her toes, even then some part of the process of forgiveness had begun, even as she flexed her knees to begin her spiteful dive.

After awhile she started to feel a little cold but she bobbed very peacefully in the water. It got colder. She began to notice how the pool seemed more like a tank, something like a miner's awful cistern. Horror Reservoir? But all was well, she told herself. Maybe if she could deal with phony bats, with practical joke bats, maybe she could learn to deal with the real thing.

Then came a real bat. It flew down to her from the purple sky, where in fact it had hovered invisibly for many minutes. She became aware of it as a wild, fluttering, papery thing that passed over the water a few feet away. Then there was another, or no, the same one repeating its flight, each time skimming nearer the water, and she took in a calm swallow of breath and tasted what felt like salty blood around her gums.

Slowly, smiling all the while but smiling idiotically, like an underwater beauty queen, working on the idea of hiding, swallowing, sewing up the phobia with the magic cartoon sewing machine, she hoisted herself up to get out of the pool. She felt that she might make it into the house. She felt that she might throw up, or fall into the barbecue and burn, or get lost wandering on the mountain. Then there was something against her neck, a light stroke, as if someone, with great delicacy and precision, had drawn the edge of an envelope across her skin—and she realized with a sickening anguish, a wave of disgust, that a bat had flown so close as actually to strike her with its wing, and that she was not ready for real bats at all, that she would very much prefer a bandeau top to one of these things. Now she wanted to dive under the water, now she wanted to scream, and then she began to run, but she didn't, but listened to the sudden, terrible sound of someone thrashing wildly in the water nearby.

Tina knew a second later that it wasn't a human being. What it was was the bat that had struck her, and it was drowning. The beauty of the deduction—her deduction—came as something extraordinary to her. It broke, in fact, her paralysis, and she took a few steps, all dripping and flushed, and switched on the pool lights, the ones that transformed the water at night into an eerie yellow aquarium. Then, after what felt like a moment of poetry, of great wisdom, she walked back slowly, breathing slowly, to the edge.

And it was there, there in the very middle of the pool, no longer thrashing and drowning but utterly still, its black wings spread out on either side of its body, like the wings of a drowned, enormous desert beetle she had once found in the kitchen sink. It gave no flinch, no spasm, no evidence of life. It did not suddenly lurch toward her when she took two or three tentative steps either away from the water or toward the water. There was no breath left in it at all.

She had murdered a defenseless bat.

And she recognized the value of that immediately. She knew right away that maybe she could use that murder to cure herself of her chiropterphobia, at least for one hour. It was so scientific, so reasonable.

Stupid bat: it must have fallen in and drowned only because it had made the mistake of brushing against her neck. She wondered that such a collision could happen, given the navigational skills everyone spoke of, but something, certainly, had gone wrong, and there was no doubt that she, Tina, had been the cause of the creature's surprising plummet and death. One thing was clear, and that was that she felt nothing for the bat. Not grief, or dread, or interest. Only energy and purpose for herself. Well, she was still afraid, but her fear became now the engine of all her new movement and strategy.

The light from the pool lit up the whole night sky like a bonfire. She went to work.

It had already occurred to her that, using the pole and scoop-net that she had already used that morning to skim off leaves and other debris from the surface of the water, she could take a poke at a dead bat—that that would be the right thing to do now, to poke at it a little, that's all. She just wanted to make contact with it.

Tina knew things about phobias. In her reading she had learned that psychiatrists use a simple plan, termed "measured approximation protocol," for combating such fears. The idea, chronicled in psychiatric journals, is for the patient to be exposed to the object of fear at ever-decreasing distances. The doctor helps the subject begin with a photograph, say, then move to a glimpse of the object from a great distance. Later, the subject is convinced to sit in the same room as the object without being able to see it, then eventually part of the object is exposed to view. Then, the subject sits closer, and finally, after carefully measured intermediate distances, the therapy is concluded with the subject actually fondling and, remarkably, even learning to love the source of fear—even learning to take hold of a living snake, in one recorded instance, and wear it every day around the neck like a favorite scarf. All this needs to be stretched out over the course of months, of course, if not years, for the typical phobic individual.

Tina knew she was not typical, that she could accelerate the process. Tina knew this: that people who had been the victims of antiphobic jokes, people who had died and come back, people who had found reserves of wisdom and forgiveness others could only dream of, were not typical. Nodding to herself gravely as she took up the pool-cleaning pole, she knew that she was superhuman. She knew that she was capable of collapsing months of approximation protocol to a matter of hours.

And, from the beginning, her plan worked well. First she walked slowly around the edge of the whole pool, taking tentative stabs at the drowned animal, screwing up the courage to make it drift a bit across the surface of the water. It was a form of indirect contact with the object of dread. And that, she decided, after ten or fifteen minutes, was the work of week number one. A very good week, a very successful session.

Week two required something a little bit more daring, but she was really up to anything now, and she boldly scooped up the bat in the net at the end of the pole and again circumnavigated the pool, this time holding the dripping, formless mammal just over the surface of the water. As she walked, watching her steps on the cement margin very carefully, because she knew she wasn't ready to fall in the pool and share it with the bat, she allowed herself a few thoughts on the subject of her roommate, about how amazed, or delighted, or confused, or even angry Claudette would be if she were to come back out at that moment and see with her own eyes what was going on.

Week three, she eventually decided, would be spent at the same pole-length distance from the object she had already established, but now the object could be brought to land and dried out. It was hard, it was horrible, but it would be no good not to go on to week three. So she took a firm new grip on the pole and maneuvered it so that the net and its contents swerved toward the barbecue, and then she stopped to let it tremble and hover over the still hot embers, like a late-night marshmallow on a skewer, and she watched grimly as, only six feet away, the steam rose delicately away from the sodden fur and bent wings, and even in the darkness, she could begin to glimpse the reality and ugliness of the creature in its natural, if deceased, condition.

There was no doubt about it. She was compressing time miraculously, but it still was all taking a very long time. At last her arms could barely hold the pole, even though she imagined—forced herself to imagine—that the animal grew progressively lighter as its burden of chlorinated water wafted away. In the end there was nothing to do but to inch her hands up a little on the pole toward its fulcrum, to make things lighter, to make it to week four.

For a moment she lost hold of rationalism. She didn't panic, but a fantasy occurred to her briefly, a daydream about how the animal might revive as the heat drew away the water and coaxed the life force to return. She remembered a demonstration in middle school science class in which a drowned, soggy fly, after being buried a while in a tiny tumulus of salt, recovered, clawed its way out of its invigorating grave, feebly shook out its wings, hesitated, and abruptly buzzed away. Thus she imagined the bat. In her daydream it slowly unfolded itself from out of its own wadded ball of leather and fur and rose vertically from the net, slowly beating a pair of now majestic and phoenixlike wings in the still hot air. But flies do not have lungs, she finally remembered, and by the time the embers were cold and her muscles dull with pain, the bat was dry, but just as dormant and dearly departed as before.

The lights stayed on in the house. Was Claudette watching the whole process from inside? Tina didn't care.

Tina was ready for week four, the most horrible of all, the week many ambitious patients never get through. Gingerly, ceremoniously, she laid the pole down on the concrete and walked slowly, tiptoe like a ballerina, toward the net. She took a breath and then, with the emotions of someone touching feces for the first time, she bent over and placed the tip of her right index finger on the very tip of what she thought was a protruding ear. It didn't move. She didn't move. She marveled at herself but was determined to go straight on from there, via shortcut, to week five.

Somewhere in the course of week five, with the breeze building from off the mountain, with the belts of stars and perhaps swarms of bats moving silently overhead, at a point where every house in the subdivision had gone dark except for theirs, Tina picked up the bat. She was dead tired, numb with cold, but she took one corner of one wing between thumb and forefinger and extracted the bat, at arm's length, from the net. Nothing remained in her to argue against the contact, but she knew that the moment held an element of magic, of ritual, of rebirth. Some people drown and die and then come back, she thought, some flies dry out in piles of salt, but how many come back as an entirely different species?

She held the dead thing before her, wing tip to wing tip, like a votary reading some holy pages. The bat matched the description that Claudette had given earlier. Its ears, bristly and vulpine, stuck out hugely from its head, and yes, absurdly enough, it wore, just above two rows of pin-sharp teeth, a mustache, an unimaginable protrusion of bubblegum-colored flesh that looked to her almost ersatz or glued on.

It was so dead. She whispered, "Poor thing," and meditated, exactly because she understood it so well now, on the horror of drowning. "You poor little guy," she sighed, and held it close enough to stare into the serenity she found in its twisted, National Geographic face. Then she laughed and realized that the process was over, and that she was finally no longer the prey of bats, but their predator.

Inside the house, Tina found Claudette already sleeping, face up on her bed with every light blazing, altogether nude, one arm thrown over her forehead, one foot still flat on the floor. At first Tina thought it would be clever to bring Claudette's joke with the bandeau top to a kind of logical conclusion, and she bent over, bat in hand, to consider how to place it on her roommate's chest. She gasped slightly, hardly believing that she was doing this, but nevertheless proceeded to carefully festoon the wings—which were in fact about the right size—over Claudette's two white breasts, creating a new and grotesque bikini, wondering dreamily to herself if this was the first time in her life she had ever played a prank on anyone. Well, it was the first time she had ever played one so piquant and imaginative, full of poetry, and symmetry, and justice.

But then she thought better of it. It was clear that the warm sensation of the skin and fur against her skin was not going to wake Claudette up from a very deep sleep, and that by morning she would certainly have rolled back and forth enough times, as sleepers do, for the bat to come off, for the joke to be spoiled. So Tina peeled the dead creature away from Claudette's bosom and, holding the ends of the wings in both hands again and standing a couple of feet back from the bed, said, in loud, deep tones, in her best imitation of Claudette's voice, "Hey Clodhopper, look out, there's a bikini top coming at you."

Her roommate stirred, but still slumbered.

Tina recited the magic words again, louder and deeper, and this time Claudette's eyelids fluttered open, and she blinked uncomprehendingly at Tina standing at the foot of her bed.

Then Tina shouted the same dumb sentence a third time, slurring the words, and lunged forward, tossing the bat awkwardly at her roommate's face, nearly stumbling and falling face first onto the mattress.

It was a bad toss, and the bat ended up on a second pillow, next to Claudette's face, positioning itself in such a way as to seem to stare sideways at her with the eyes of a forlorn puppy.

As it happened, Claudette at that moment had been working through the plot of an extravagant and vivid dream. She was working where she really worked, at the college, and she was doing what she really sometimes had to do, unlocking the supply cabinets to get at some new staples and notepads for her desk. But there was something strange. The department secretary was there in the room with a stiletto, saying she had to open the mailbag, and when she ripped it apart scores of tiny Mexican teacup dogs, all either dead or perhaps asleep, spilled out everywhere. When, in the artificial light of the bedside lamp, Claudette opened her eyes from this minute dream and squinted, still half-dreaming, at the mustachioed bat flying toward her and landing on the pillow, she wasn't at all surprised, because she was still halfway back in the dream, and she thought that the bat was just one of those little Mexican dogs spilled out from the bag. Then, when sleep and dream dissolved and she realized what the little mammal really was, she sat up straight, and laughed. She laughed and coughed so long and hard that Tina had time to measure the laughter, and judge it. It was unbelievable, but she could see that Claudette knew the whole story. Her clever roommate had quickly inferred the mar-

velous process of approximation and cure, and found it all very typical, very droll.

This moment of insight really seemed like the second miracle of
the night. But Tina was wiser than she had been a few hours before,
and she understood as she backstepped slowly out of the room that
Claudette's laughter spoke only partially of congratulations, of celebration and delight, and that there was a harshness to it as well, a
laughing to scorn. And although she wouldn't have said that she had
hoped for equilibrium, that she had wished her inverted gag to bring
about a rebirth of friendship, it was clear now that no balance or
negotiation could ever be reached. It was too bad, but Claudette's
laughter and Tina's retreat only held the promise of a hundred smart
affronts, and a hundred mutual indignities, to come.

Planet
of the
Evangelists

In the apartment on Revolución she inherited from her murdered father, Tyrsa Echeverria lived alone and dispirited in the city of Hermosillo, surrounded by the poinsettias and marigolds that kept arriving for days and days after the funeral. Every morning after coffee and bread, finally provoked out of her lethargy by the painful smell of the flowers, she walked twelve blocks to a small *secundaria* in the fashionable section of the city, where she taught grammar and business correspondence. Her well-heeled students were for the most part spoiled and ambitionless, and she referred to them, though they were only a little younger than herself, as the "tiny stupids." Her teaching, while unenthusiastic, was full of entertaining artificialities: comic grimaces and witty jokes on students that made her one of the most popular teachers—among the other teachers.

And during those long hours when she taught and joked and disdained, she kept three-quarters of her mind on her father's murder, and the memory of it and fact of it came close to suffocating her. "They will kill me," her father the journalist had told her, three days before the murder, referring to any and all of the powerful *licenciados* he had satirized. "They'll kill me because I tell the truth about them. Then you'll have to tell the truth, Tyrsa. That will be better, really, because they'd never kill a woman."

But Tyrsa told no truths, wrote no letters. After his death she simply moved into his apartment, continued teaching, and waited for the episodes of suffocation to end.

Then one day, near the end of the winter semester, her mother wrote her to announce her remarriage.

On a Saturday afternoon that poured dreary yellow light through the windows, Tyrsa read the letter rapidly, then used both hands to crumple the lavender paper to the size and shape of a lavender snowball. Five minutes or ten minutes later, she lit a cigarette.

"My mother has moved to a different planet," she explained out loud, as if speaking to students. "You might come to the conclusion that the memory of my father has been betrayed. But no. She is only getting on a spaceship and moving to a different planet, in a different solar system."

The wedding announcement enclosed with the letter was a gloomy and Victorian production with an oval photograph of the new couple rotogravured onto heavy card stock, their names printed below in bristling Germanic letters. Tyrsa gazed at the gloomy portrait a long time, astonished by the expense and mawkishness of it all. She would have cried—if crying were something she could do easily—for her father, a man too clever and therefore too hated by the powerful to afford such lavishness. "A man too good," she continued in her lecturer's voice, "to have received any reward but murder, much less public recognition, in such an unbalanced and immoral world."

But she could not let go of the announcement. She had the urge to crumple it as she had crumpled the letter, but realized the card stock was too thick. Finally she lit another cigarette, fumbling the lighter awkwardly, thought for a moment, then walked into the kitchen and placed the card, which by that time had soiled her fingertips somewhat with its coat of thick black ink, face down in an empty wastebasket, along with the lavender snowball.

"I will not burn this card or this letter," she announced, and walked away, and was proud of her restraint, but came back later with two overflowing ashtrays from the coffee table and dumped their bitter powder into the wastebasket, burying the new husband's face like the face of a miner entombed by a cave-in, a face swallowed in the darkness at the bottom of a well.

This was a satisfactory burial. She laughed lightly and capered in a little circle around the wastebasket with her arms held gracefully above her head. Perhaps it had the approximate appearance of the dance of a shaman around a fetish or a bonfire, but it was in fact no more than the half-angry, half-satiric circle she would sometimes make around her desk while some poor student (whom she had made sit on the edge of her desk after an especially idiotic response) squirmed and blushed and buried his face in his arms and disappeared from public view, like the newlyweds at the bottom of the wastebasket.

When she finished her dance she felt sick to her stomach, and she sat down heavily on the kitchen floor, setting her palms down among the bread crumbs she had not swept up for days. Then she did cry, and, at the end of crying, swore she would not live in that apartment, or even in Hermosillo, for another hour.

"I will go work in California for a while," she said with great conviction, drying her tears with a dishtowel. She had never thought of such a thing before, but she convinced herself without effort that it was something she had always wanted to do. Immediately the whole future constructed itself quite intricately before her eyes. After all, it would be quite easy. She could live with her cousin up there, earn a North American salary, and get away from the reform school and the students. Somewhere over the rainbow, she thought. If her mother could travel to another planet, then why couldn't she?

Several days later she coolly announced this surprising plan to her students and her colleagues and even the director of the school, and then, because they all expected her to go, she had to go.

She had some money saved, so things did not go badly, and there were no great complications or physical risks in becoming an illegal alien, as she somewhat contemptuously realized was the case for many others. The border town of Mexilindo was one bus ride and one pack of cigarettes away, and from there she called her cousin Soraida the American citizen, with whom she had already arranged things, to come and pick her up and smuggle her across.

That was certainly the worst part of it. Soraida, laughing and daubing tears from her eyes at the sight of her childhood friend, drove her to a deserted part of Mexilindo, opened the trunk of her Subaru, pushed Tyrsa and her bag down inside the awful space, and firmly slammed down the lid with cheery exclamations of apology and good luck.

"This is how," Soraida yelled to her through the keyhole, "I did what you're doing six years ago."

But the words were not a consolation to Tyrsa. For the next two hours she curled herself into herself a hundred times, bent herself pathetically in the darkness like a folding chair, and could not help but breathe in the stink of the car exhaust and the rubber of the spare tire and the sweet raspberry smell of spilled transmission fluid, while the small of her back, where her blouse had hiked up, rubbed helplessly against the edge of something vibrating and very hot. All the while Soraida kept the radio on loud to broadcast the fact that she was still at the wheel and that all was well, but Tyrsa could not help but think she had made a bad decision, and that the lid of the trunk would ultimately open to reveal a nightmare North America: a landscape, she imagined, of spilled chemicals and pillars of petroleum smoke, a field of fires tended by poor black men who slept each night in the trunks of tiny cars.

But an hour later, when the lid finally did open, there was nothing like that. The world that unfolded to her outside the trunk of the car was green and smelled of coming rain. There were pastel, almost Mexican-style houses, and, on each side of the street, beautiful to see, a row of palm trees so tall their fronds looked tiny as mint leaves.

And that was all there was to it: she had reached the end of a second-rate immigration ordeal, nothing to compare to most such ordeals, and all that remained was to float into her cousin's pastel house, where she drank a cup of Mexican coffee and smoked an American cigarette, while Soraida got on the phone and started calling around to track down some kind of job.

It took exactly five hours for Soraida to find Tyrsa a position as a housekeeper. Her employers were Frederick and Bella Montgomery, a quiet, fiftyish couple who lived on an old, jacaranda-lined avenue of Luxorville, and it was Tyrsa's job to come and clean their four bedrooms and two bathrooms and spruce and dust things up every day before Soraida came to pick her up at five o'clock.

It was not hard work. The Montgomerys gave precise but friendly instructions in nearly fluent Spanish, assured her that her illegal status was their closely guarded secret, then disappeared to their distant, mysterious jobs, leaving Tyrsa to go for days at a time without seeing either of them, a circumstance which struck her as extraordinary and somehow unforgivable. Every day by two the work of scrubbing and cleaning, and finally of dusting the Montgomerys' collection of clocks and porcelain owls, was finished. The house, clean beyond clean, demanded nothing more of her, and she used the rest of the day to relax and reread the only book she had thought to bring along on the journey, a very long and rather tiresome novel by Pérez Galdós. But even with all that, she felt uncomfortable and, in the back of her mind, vaguely ashamed of herself for having abandoned her incorrigible but after all needy students. And why? Why had she done it? Earning a good but not spectacular salary at a rather demeaning job did not seem now like a motive. And what about escaping the sphere of a mother and stepfather whom she had to admit, after all, were utterly powerless? What about running away from two pitiful individuals who most likely were at that moment, at all moments, disintegrating, coming apart completely, each one respectively undone by the guilt of having chased an innocent daughter so far away?

Daughter's estrangement from mother dated from a gruesome Monday, one day after the funeral of the martyred father. Tyrsa was barely breathing, barely conscious under the weight of her grief, drifting carelessly and pointlessly from one corner of the apartment to the other, haunted by a dream she had had the night before that her father had returned from the grave to show her another letter to the editor he was writing, this one implausibly naming the Church of Rome as his murderer and asking her to revenge his death through papal assassination. Unfortunately she walked into the kitchen unannounced and unperceived, only to find the widow deep in breathy conversation and hand in hand with Humberto Ostragón, a little-known but egotistical TV figure who made a living doing weekly voice-overs for Brazilian soap operas. The two of them, Humberto and Catalina, took shape before her eyes as they probably had appeared for years (had Tyrsa the wits to see it), as lovers. But the sight and comprehension of that secret at that moment blinded Tyrsa temporarily and she stumbled against the telephone on the wall, knocking the receiver noisily to the floor. The lovers yelped and separated themselves clumsily, but Tyrsa recomposed herself like a gracious loser and was even urbane enough to wish the couple an icy congratulations. Then she turned gracefully on her heels, walked away, and determined to go out of her mother's life for the next several hundred years.

But it was Catalina who went out of her daughter's life the next day. Tyrsa did not pay much attention to the letters that followed—breezy, oblivious paragraphs detailing the couple's travels in Brazil, their elaborate vitamin regime, their purchase of a burgundy Aplausa with the money Ostragón earned from his work on the most popular *telenovela* of the year.

It all fell apart. A few weeks after returning to Hermosillo, Humberto and Catalina broke up, and Tyrsa, with all the solemn majesty of a prophet, understood that she and her mother would get together again, and visit the tomb of the martyred father, and dress in widow's weeds, and let loose the mutual flood of tears at last. She even believed herself capable then of reviving the martyr's campaign, of writing some new letters to the editor, just as he had forsworn her to do.

Then came the wedding announcement. The couple had patched up their differences. It had taken a miracle, but they would marry and be happy after all.

After working at the Montgomerys' for two months Tyrsa realized that she detested doing housework for other people, especially people whom she hardly ever saw, and she could not see how it would be possible to tolerate two years of such unrelenting physical repetition. She tried an infinity of techniques to break up the monotony of scrubbing and wiping and vacuuming, but to no effect. The tedium of it all was insurmountable. She found herself taking on a strong but inexplicable dislike to the whole United States, or "This Planet," as she called it, even though so far she had seen no more than the Montgomerys' manicured, jacaranda-lined avenue and Soraida's somewhat shabbier, palm-lined avenue, and the commercial, very Mexicanized boulevard in between. One day she complained about all this to her cousin, who had started out as a housekeeper and now worked as a secretary, but Soraida almost died laughing at her bitter outburst. Daubing the corners of her eyes, she suggested to Tyrsa that if she would stick it out they could go back home together with enough money to buy a little hotel, maybe on a resort lake somewhere, where North Americans like the Montgomerys could come and the two of them could indirectly get their revenge by way of rotten service and subtly poisoned food. So Tyrsa laughed at her cousin's nonsense, and sighed, and swallowed her distaste, and decided the only thing to do was to improve herself.

First she gave up smoking. Then she cleaned the house so vigorously every morning that she was done by noon and could spend the rest of the day lying on the living room couch and switching from Pérez Galdós to an English-as-a-second-language text Soraida had loaned her, something called *America Is a Rich Tapestry*—short essays followed by lists of very challenging, very thought-provoking comprehension questions.

Then the visitors, the ringers of the musical doorbell, started to come. For weeks there had been nothing, and then it seemed as if there was some incomprehensible stranger coming by the house almost every afternoon. Finally, here was something she liked about her job. After all the pointless mopping and long, dead-quiet afternoons, it was suddenly very entertaining to answer the door and find there maybe a mailman with a package that wouldn't fit through the slot, a Boy Scout or a soldier selling tickets to some event, a blind man selling brooms, a hobo who wanted to freshen the paint of the house numbers on the curb. Best of all were the Mormon boys with their beautiful Spanish and preposterous illustrations of a long-haired Jesus among Mexican pyramids, looking like nothing so much as the German hippies she got so sick of when once she took her students on a field trip to Teotihuacán.

One day she opened the door to find a very skinny black teenager who explained to her that he was trying to find people to pay him to run in a race: for every mile he ran, a cancer patient somewhere would receive an hour of radiation therapy. Tyrsa understood scarcely any of it, was a little afraid of the boy (perhaps not exactly because he was black but because he talked so fast and never smiled, though she remembered with some nervousness her vision of the black men tending fires), and she shut the door in his face in midsentence and then felt terrible about it all afternoon. The next day, as she lay reading a strange essay which claimed, as best she could make out, that ownership of guns ought to be legalized but that all gun users ought to be shot by a firing squad, the doorbell rang its musical phrase again and this time it was a red-haired young woman with a clipboard and a patient way of repeating everything she said. For the first time Tyrsa felt she could understand the English language, and when it became apparent that the young lady's paper was a petition that called for banning the ownership of guns, she was amazed by the coincidence. Smiling and gesturing, she showed the petitioner the book in her hand and pointed to the essay she had been reading, and they both laughed and Tyrsa kept saying, "Too funny, too funny."

Then she felt unbearably sad, because she could really go no further in the conversation, and she slowly, slowly closed the heavy white door, nodding her head enthusiastically in the narrowing crack all the while, and finally, with the door closed, she felt angry, unspeakably angry at a planet that smothered her, an atmosphere that deadened her tongue and filled her with a sense of second childhood and second, tiny stupidity.

The next day Tyrsa was sleeping when the doorbell rang, and she opened the door with a yawn and a strand of hair in her eye, half-expecting the gun girl to have come back.

Instead her eyes gradually focused on a figure in suit and tie, a man she immediately didn't like the looks of. It was someone she would have closed the door on, if she were not still feeling guilty about having done just that to the black teenager.

At first all she could notice about him was his funny head: a dome crisscrossed by purple canals, a pair of big, red, Anglo-Saxon ears. But it was not this figure that made her hesitate but the teenage girl who had come with him and who stood several yards behind, hesitating and shy in the driveway. The man had started talking immediately but Tyrsa stared and stared over his shoulder because the girl, black-haired as a Mexican and just as beautiful, seemed to be peering directly at her, and she had never seen eyes with a story to tell quite like those before. These were eyes that said, along with the poorly fitting dress and downturned mouth, I am in dark trouble and can you please help me. Please please help me.

But all the time the bald man was talking louder in his rapid, bewildering English and Tyrsa turned to him and forgot the girl, or put her at the back of her mind for just a moment. But what was the old fellow talking about? She couldn't really follow, just glanced nervously at the purple filigree across his scalp, his way of rubbing a palm across it as he spoke, as if he were greasing down remembered hair. She thought he looked like an American movie star whose name she couldn't remember. A moment later she decided he looked a little like the elderly Cantinflas, but only because he had the same gray mustache and double chin. His story, as near as she could make out, was a terrible one—like the girl's?—but clearly his idea was that she should listen to this dark story with sympathy and recognition and finally joy. But all Tyrsa could think of as she stared into her own frowning reflection in the man's heavy eyeglasses was her father's nearly identical pair, which she inherited but had left behind in Hermosillo, and a wave of grief came back, and she thought of how he finally got pushed down a flight of stairs, and how he ended up with the cerebral hemorrhage, all because of his giant vocabulary and the way he wrote and wrote, just like this visitor talked, except that with her father she knew what he was saying all the time, about to hell with the ruling party, to hell with the priests, and to hell especially with the landlords, and no way will I stop writing my letters to the editor, until, like she warned him, like he warned her, he ended up dead.

"You come in please?" she screeched suddenly, trying to drown out the terrible images in her mind by reconcentrating on the man's incessant talk. She had the urge to try to capture this pair of visitors, to make them sit down in the Montgomerys' living room, on the

Montgomerys' furniture, and bring them coffee and find out why the girl needed help and to make the man repeat what he was saying, only this time slower, slower, so she could figure out what it was he was doing to the girl, what hypnosis he was maybe guilty of. So she could forget about Mexico.

But the bald man smiled and said very sweetly, very slowly, No Thank You. He then turned and gestured impatiently at the girl and suddenly there she was inches from Tyrsa, her eyes broadcasting the same strange SOS, except now even more intentionally, more heartbreakingly.

It was terrible. Tyrsa felt like she had fallen down a hole with the girl, that their bodies pressed against each other at the bottom of the well and that somehow they had no voices and could not shout for help. She thought and thought, and wanted somehow to insist on her invitation to come inside, but the ice-breaking, sociable words weren't there, and all she could say was "you are come in please," again, but not as violently this time and the man smiled and shook his head so forcefully she could hear his neck scraping against his starched white collar. She wanted so much to speak in Spanish, and even suspected that the girl might know Spanish, but she felt foolish and rude to do so and kept her mouth shut. Finally Tyrsa could do no more than to funnel all her powers of concentration, all the propaganda that used to work on her students, into a fierce, wonderfully piteous smile, which she hoped was a smile that could be secretly latched on to, and remembered, and returned to. The girl expressionlessly thrust a piece of folded paper forward and Tyrsa took the opportunity to grab the girl's hand and give it a squeeze—and she believed from what felt like a fleeting squeeze in return that her communication had been understood. Then they were gone, marching in strange unison down the sidewalk, leaving Tyrsa at the door with the paper clutched to her bosom, noticing for the first time, only when the couple was nearly out of sight, far down the sidewalk, that they were dressed in an identical blue fabric, and that the man's strong odor, which she now identified as cologne, still hung in the air around the porch, and that the afternoon in Luxorville was suddenly very overcast and a light rain had begun to come down, turning the jacarandas into soft lavender clouds.

"Beloved Tyrsa," the lavender letter had read, "beloved daughter, I want you to be the first to know of my happiness."

There was no need for a cigarette. Tyrsa noted how this was a time she once would have needed one. But she turned like a sleepwalker and drifted heavily toward the sofa, wondering off and on about the teenager and how they had maybe communicated with each other, maybe not, thinking how funny it was that she had wished for a little more noise and company in the house but when it had come it had just rattled her and made her feel worse, and that starting tomorrow she was going to look for another job.

Later, collapsed on the sofa, almost asleep, she remembered the paper, and unfolded it close to her eyes, and read aloud to herself, barely comprehending here and there, the old, thorny English: "All have sinned . . . there is not a just man upon earth . . . We are all as an unclean thing . . . filthy rags . . . The heart is deceitful above all things, and desperately wicked."

At the bottom it was signed, in the tiniest letters, "The Reverend Livermore," and that of course had to be the bald gentleman's name. It was funny to her for a moment: Cantinflas in the role of the Reverend Livermore. Then she refolded the paper, depressed and at the same time interested in the whole sordid business, the phenomenon of American evangelists. Her ESL book had an interesting reading on creationism versus evolution, and she picked it up and started skimming it again. Hallelujahs, they were called in Hermosillo. Her father, she thought she remembered, had once written a letter to the editor about them, accusing them of plotting with the Catholics to distribute cocaine to Mexican schoolchildren, to send an addicted Mexico back to the dark ages. Something like that. But she was having trouble concentrating. She could picture right then only Ostragón and the smudged rotogravure of the happy couple, the way his thinning hair had been airbrushed to look thicker and younger and blacker than it was.

What it was that she finally wanted after all her sighing and day-dreaming on the sofa was for the two Americans, the Svengali and his slave-girl, to come back, not only because she was worried about the girl, but because she needed someone to help her out with her Mexican reverie. In her daydream, she saw herself rescuing the girl and fleeing with her back to Mexico. They would bring Soraida with them, and they could start the hotel right away, with whatever money they had. The girl would do the cooking and cleaning, and everything would be absolutely perfect.

Tyrsa suddenly bounded from the sofa, stretched her hands up toward the ceiling, and floated fancifully, like an amateur ballerina, across the living room to the mantle, where she picked up one of the Montgomerys' porcelain owls. It was a wise, cartoonish owl wearing glasses and a black graduation cap, and she slipped it into the pocket of her apron. Something inside her had awoken, a switch had been flicked on, and she felt like taking over the Montgomerys' house, of becoming the director there. It was not enough, she realized, to wait for the girl to come back. She would have to rescue her, that was certain. And after the rescue she wouldn't let go of her prize, her victory, no matter what. She would save one girl from the dark ages, and someone—perhaps her father—ought to be proud.

And in fact when she got out into the rain she saw that the mysterious pair had only advanced a few houses down. Livermore was on the porch, deep in conversation with an elderly resident, and the girl—whom she suspected now more than ever to be some kind of Mexican or Chicana—had been left behind again on the sidewalk, and stood there with her shoulders bent, eyes on the ground, one toe of one shoe moving idly among the fallen blossoms. She was apparently waiting for her cue to come forward and hand out the literature, or perhaps she was thinking of running away right then and there, though she looked neither left nor right, and Tyrsa thought, She is every bit as stupid as my tiny stupids.

Still, it seemed imperative to march straight forward, take the uneducated girl in her arms, whisper stern Spanish reassurances to her, and take her back to the house, back to the Montgomerys', where they would wait for Soraida to rescue them.

But Tyrsa didn't move, perhaps because for an instant she had recalled something she already knew quite well, a remark a teacher had made to her once when, as a brazen child, she lied that she hadn't done her homework because her father had died: that often the mind creates or at least embroiders stories that in some ways we do better to believe. Maybe the poor girl was no sex slave but only a shy but stupidly satisfied volunteer, content to shuffle along in the service of some bland Protestantism. Maybe the old man was even her father.

Then there was something else to consider, Tyrsa told herself, taking a step backwards. There was all the potential trouble that she could get into, the risk of getting involved in some legal dispute when she herself was, after all, illegal. She could certainly not afford to be interviewed by police or authorities of any kind. Maybe better, she thought with a rush of relief, turning away already, maybe better to forget the idiotic creature who stood only thirty steps down the sidewalk awaiting a doom which might be no worse than Tyrsa's own doom, the doom of simply being caught up in some temporary and worldly sadness, with every opportunity of escaping to something else if the weight and grief and atmosphere became too much.

"Let her move to another planet like I did," Tyrsa mumbled as she danced up the steps to the Montgomerys' house. "Let her lie in the trunk of a car for two hours if she wants to get away."

And she went back inside. Trembling a little, pleased with her resolution, but retaining just enough sadness and sense of failure to make her press one sweaty palm uncomfortably hard against her forehead and the other against a slightly accelerated heartbeat, Tyrsa lay down on the couch again, picked up her English textbook, opened it at random, and read, "By far the best way to learn English is to establish a close relationship with an American."

"And so my dear child," the lavender letter had read, "despite your hatefulness and disobedience, your future stepfather and I have made a special place for you in our hearts."

Suddenly Tyrsa was off the couch and down on her knees, determined to pray. It was impossible for her to speak to God, so she spoke to her father, because, in his letters to the editor, he praised the poor as saints and hated the devils who kept all the power.

"Dear Father, who is in heaven," she pronounced, "I pray to you, if you have any influence left at all, to save that poor girl, who through love of a false God has fallen into the hands of a Svengali, a terrible old man, a decrepit hallelujah. If you can, give her the intelligence to escape. Do you understand that? Shower her with some kind of intelligence and, I don't know, science and light?"

That's when there was a knock on the door. Tyrsa fell prostrate on the carpet and moaned. No one had ever knocked before. They had always played the music of the doorbell. She didn't move but stopped moaning and began to nod wisely, and listen. The hollow, drumlike patter, a savage hammering against the hard wet wood, said help me help me help me help. Tyrsa wanted to do some rescuing, God knows, but Tyrsa was tired, Tyrsa was terrified. She wondered suddenly if prayers were real, and spirits listened. She wondered, alternately, if Reverend Livermore had noticed her following him and had now come racing back, escorted by a goon squad of immigration authorities and TV evangelists.

But then she could not stop herself from scrambling to her feet and rushing to the door to at least see who it was. As it happened there was a tiny glass peephole in the door that she normally didn't like to use, and through it Tyrsa, on tiptoe, had a clear, fish-eyed preview of the Victim. There she was, a caricature of terror, like something out of a silent movie. Her eyes were rolling in her skull, then comically darting back and forth from the door, which she seemed to be imploring to open, and the sidewalk behind her, which she seemed to expect shortly to reveal her persecutor. Her hands were clutched below her breasts in a gesture of stomach pain, or self-defense.

So prayer does bring results, she noted to herself with the calm sensation of having made a useful discovery. The girl had run away from her evangelist and had come to her, to Tyrsa, the Mexican teacher turned housecleaner with the round, intelligent eyes. Who else in this neighborhood, after all, would ever, could ever, help some dummy out of a pentecostal nightmare? So when Tyrsa did at last open the door the tiniest bit the girl seemed to shrink herself into exactly the width of the crack and slipped inside in an instant, robbed of language for the moment but gesturing at Tyrsa to close the door behind her and then, when the door was closed, scraping at the housecleaner with youthful, frightfully aggressive fingers.

"No te preocupes," muttered Tyrsa, guiding the fugitive erratically, pushing her first toward the stairway, then the kitchen, then the living room sofa, all the while prancing away a little from the girl's painful scratching nails.

"Oh," sighed the girl, finding her voice as she lay down. Then, contrary to what Tyrsa had expected, she spoke in English, but only to say, over and over, "He is not a Christian. He is not a Christian."

Tyrsa could understand this simple, repetitive ESL but at first took it literally and thought it meant that Livermore was some kind of Hindu, or Jew. Then she realized that the girl was trying to say that her abductor was no gentleman, that his religiosity revolved, as Tyrsa had suspected all afternoon, around sex.

By the time the girl ceased her litany and lay motionless, Tyrsa knew very well how she would succeed in the United States. She would work as a housekeeper just long enough to earn a credential and then resume her career as a teacher, the only difference being that her students would be American teenagers, and she would help them emerge from their labyrinths of sex and stupidity.

"Oh, you unbelievable child," Tyrsa screamed in Spanish at the trembling figure that stretched out like a stick doll on the sofa. "How could you let yourself get involved with them? What do you expect me to do for you? Am I your mother, to get you out of every jam you get yourself into?" Then in slow careful English she said, "All has sinned. Yo repito. All has sinned."

Then, on an inspiration, she took the wise little owl out of her apron pocket and held it in front of the girl's eyes, like a priest brandishing a cross.

"I am a teacher," she said, relaxing and smiling, breathing deeply. "A Teacher." Then, as she would often do for the benefit of her students, she began to beat out with her feet some rhythms of her old dance. She danced, and raised the magic intellectual owl above her head, high-stepping slowly, cranelike, around the sofa, continuing all the while to berate the girl at the top of her voice, her tongue set free to speak the vilest, wittiest names she knew.

An
Aztec
Sphinx

———

Two guys boil up a dinner of broccoli and green beans and gummy brown rice, so much garlic salt on top that they burn the edges of their tongues, then decide to skip writing their assignments and get high.

"Close your eyes," commands Tyler from across the table, face lit by a candle, eyes narrow and bland. "Now, listen to me and imagine yourself a skin diver, like what was that guy's name? Lloyd Bridges. Grab onto the arm of your chair and visualize that arm—view it in your mind's eye, now—as a branch of coral. No wait, coral is sharp. It's always sharp as a razor to Lloyd Bridges. He always veers sharply away from coral."

In the middle of this lecture, which might lead to laughter were

Tyler not so exacting and passionless in his warnings and Brad so green and desperate to learn to do all this right, the telephone, perhaps a little like the warning bell of the skin diver's boat, sounds, and Tyler is closest.

Outside it is not really dark because the sky is full of plain flat clouds that reflect back the light of the town, and the mountains surrounding the basin aren't dark like mountains but more like yellowish, luminescent banks of dirt.

"Nothing but a dial tone," Tyler mumbles from where he stands near the glass doors looking down at the parking lot, holding the receiver away from his ear, his fingers to his mouth as though about to throw up. "Nothing but this dial tone. Nothing but the tone of the dial."

Then a long space of time elapses. Tyler's face, normally mandarin and smooth as wood, has taken on a kind of recklessness, and in fact he stands staring in the middle of the living room for a long time, trembling slightly, his fingertips resting on either side of his throbbing neck and his eyes tilted upward to fix on the granules of the cottage-cheese ceiling. When he ultimately speaks again his eyes revolve dramatically, like those of an angry professor, before they finally fix on Brad, whose eyes, like a student's, are apathetic and still submarine.

"Tomorrow, Brad," he says in a voice so serious and sepulchral that Brad wonders if he is going to announce his suicide, "tomorrow we will quit school. Tomorrow we will go and get that job in Mexico."

It's 1982, they are college students, and neither has started to write the book report on *Oedipus Rex* that is due in their English composition class by one o'clock tomorrow.

Brad squirms in his seat and lets his hands glide to his bare knees, where they dance nervously for a while, like dry leaves.

Brad almost always wears cut-offs, even in winter. Speaking generally, he is more casual and witty than Tyler. They are the same age but Brad always seems somehow newer to the world, somehow the baby. He wears glasses like John Lennon's and has a little crater in his forehead, shaped like a three-quarter moon, that looks like a sports injury but is in fact congenital.

There is some kind of job in Mexico. Yesterday, at a table in the quad, they were given literature about a factory position fifty miles south, just over the border in what the man called a "modern and comfortable" town, newly created "out of dust and poverty," and named La Fábrica del Pueblo, thereafter referred to by Brad as El Pueblo de la Fábrica. He calls it that because he hates it. But late at night in the apartment, still holding his breath, still clutching the arms of his chair, it seems bizarrely inevitable to him that they go, and, with a heavy, loutish, skin diver's nod, Brad signals an imperturbable agreement, then exhales so hard he blows out the candle.

But an hour of darkness does not pass before they both realize, even before they come down from the general persuasiveness of their marijuana high, that in fact their plan is sophomoric and probably doomed. In a new, relatively straightened state of mind, they begin to speak or think differently. Doesn't it seem crazy just to breeze down to Mexico to work? Isn't the economy, after all, much worse than ours at its worst? Don't even the best jobs, like doctor, like engineer, pay hardly anything at all?

The man in the quad was a middle-aged American, a hippie really, dressed up like a Mexican Indian, like a Mayan or something, all white cotton and embroideries, who spoke of "solidarity with the Mexican worker" and "restoration of the environment" and told them that they would earn five dollars an hour and not have to work too hard for it.

"Not that I'm backing out," groans Brad finally, at exactly two in the morning. They are standing on the balcony, breathing what feels like pure oxygen. "But didn't the guy say that it was a kind of clean-up thing? What does 'clean-up' mean? That might mean toxic waste clean-up, or something like that."

"I imagine it is toxic," says Tyler, testily. It is a truth about him that he does not permit himself, ever, to admit he has made a poor suggestion. He is lying on his mattress in the corner of the living room, listening to something through his headphones so symphonic and loud that Brad can almost identify it from across the room.

"What is that you're listening to?" he mutters but his roommate hears nothing, just continues to talk.

"If it weren't toxic, or nuclear, or something hazardous, do you think they would pay five dollars an hour?" Here his voice takes on a grating volume that Brad thinks is more an effect of paranoia than of speaking over the music. "Five dollars an hour is a fortune for those guys down there. And it's pretty good for us too, considering that there isn't a single job here that pays more than four-fifty. Listen, Brad. We'll go work for one day, earn our forty dollars, and then catch a bus south. We just need to get started, and then we can go down down down, if you want. We can even get as far as the pyramids on a forty-dollar bus ticket. Isn't that what you want?"

"Not just the pyramids," sighs Brad.

"Brad, you've ended up reading more about those cultures than I ever did. Why is it that the ancient Mexicans built pyramids but never—it sounds silly I know—never a sphinx?"

"I firmly believe . . . I firmly believe that there is a sphinx," says Brad, getting an ugly, postmarijuana picture of it in his mind. This is not a sculpture but a living menacing being, a jaguar perhaps, with a saturnine and thinly mustachioed man's face—the face of the man in the quad. "This sphinx has not yet been discovered."

"Oh Christ—what about school?" groans Tyler, an hour later, just as a streak of yellow-gray light is visible over the tops of the other apartment buildings. By now they are both lying on their backs on the cold concrete of the balcony. "What about our book reports?"

But that seems to Brad like the least of their worries. Later, after a couple of early morning beers and phone calls, Tyler proclaims, as if in victory, that they can sublet the apartment to a girl named Sarah, and then they have to do it, they have to go work in Mexico.

Sarah comes over in the late morning and Tyler introduces her as his girlfriend. As far as Brad is concerned, it is very uncharacteristic of his roommate not to mention a love affair, and he coldly begins to believe that Tyler is considering a secretly truncated trip to Mexico, not the virtual immigration and pioneerlike settlement that Brad so easily imagines.

But Sarah is so funny and attractive that Brad warms up. She cautiously sips from a beer bottle like a child with a first bottle of soda and ignores Tyler's overly detailed lectures about watering plants and forwarding mail. Instead she tells Brad a joke.

"How many leftist ideologues does it take to screw in a light bulb?"

"How many?"

"That's not funny!"

She is small and precise and asks, when she spills a little beer, for a *servilleta* instead of a napkin, and Brad is jealous because he realizes that she is in fact pretty much stunning with her tiny round sunglasses and a thin brown cotton dress that features a lace collar and a row of old-fashioned horn buttons down the front. When Tyler bends down solemnly to kiss his girl good-bye, Brad walks a few steps away to give them some privacy but finds himself glancing back to get a last look. The dress, seen from that distance, is the color of seaweed, he thinks, and then he imagines her for a moment having stepped out of the sea, like Aphrodite, clothed only in shimmering strips of algae.

He feels ashamed to gaze, to participate that way in their love scene, but Tyler and Sarah ignore him, or don't care what he sees, and they kiss and hungrily kiss again, not like nineteen but like fifteen-year-olds, until Brad finally sets off on his own and walks half the way to the freeway on-ramp before he hears the thud of Tyler's boots racing up the sidewalk behind him, feels on his shoulder the weight of Tyler's hand, which he shrugs off and walks faster and faster and faster.

Two guys try to hitchhike. But hitchhiking, by 1982, has become nearly impossible. Perhaps one driver out of a thousand will stop to give young college-age males a ride. By the time they get picked up it is almost dusk, and the driver will only take them as far as an A-Okay campground a few miles from the border, in the middle of the alfalfa fields. By the time they get there they feel dirty, and what they can make out in the dark does not look nice. The camping area is paved with asphalt, with no cushion of lawn or even dirt in sight. Tyler points out to Brad that the place has been established on the grounds of an old drive-in movie theater. No screen or speakers remain, but the ground still undulates in long parallel ridges, and the office and lavatories are housed in a battered and rusty Quonset hut that Tyler theorizes was once the projection room and snack bar.

Brad feels sick. He slams down his pack on the rock-hard blacktop and trudges to the men's room, only to find that it is locked, out of order. He sneaks into the women's lavatory. There he finds that he can theorize as well as Tyler.

"This stall has been used by men," he says aloud, "because the paint on the bottom edges of the dividers is peeling away, and this must be due to thousands of splashes of urine, of uric acid."

He has trouble passing water. Finally, impatient, he glances down at his unresponsive organ and freezes, for a moment, with fright. It's strange and stupid, but he has forgotten to close the Swiss army knife that he keeps dangling from a belt loop and the main blade, cold and sharp as a samurai's sword because he has been working on it with a whetstone all day while waiting for a ride, is pressed up directly against the shaft of his exposed and suddenly urine-blasting penis. The image is so horrible—it reminds him of, but is much more gruesome than, the movie they have both recently seen in their English composition class, where a razor blade slices open an eye—that he reacts with a start and brushes the blade away so quickly that he cuts the thumb on his left hand.

At first there is no pain, not even a sensation, and when at last he gets the blade folded away and holds up his thumb to take a look at it he is surprised to see a very deep and horizontal cut, halfway between the tip of the thumb and the joint. As he watches, fascinated, the cut fills with blood, and more blood, and the blood is dripping everywhere. Several great drops of blood, the size of cranberries, plop into the toilet bowl and mingle with his urine there.

Tyler walks into the restroom and busies himself at a sink, playing with the spring-loaded faucet that will only release one eruption of cold water at a time. Brad's pain has come on slowly, then explosively, like a headache that comes from a blow, and although by then he has sat down on the toilet and decided to keep the accident a secret, the pain eventually turns so fierce—it feels like the knife has severed hard layers of muscle and heavy bundles of nerves—that he closes the door of the stall and half groans, half squeals.

"Brad, is that you?" yells Tyler over a noisy blast of water, his voice liquidly and garbled with toothpaste.

Then Tyler, unsatisfied with the silence, taps on the door of the stall. Brad is ready for him. He flings the door open, smiles up at his friend, and holds up the bloody thumb, its wound still compressed by the other thumb, for an uncaring world to see.

"I have managed to butcher my thumb, Tyler," he says, laughing at Tyler's apathetic face. Then he laughs at himself.

"Oh World Oh Life Oh Time," he adds with a shrug. "Oh, *yeah*. Now do me a favor, Tyler, and go buy a Band-Aid in the minimart."

"Hold it," says Tyler. "Think for a minute, Bro. Can you really buy just one Band-Aid? I think I'll have to get us a whole box. Don't you think it might be better to just drive into town and find a doctor? I wouldn't be surprised if you need three or four stitches in that thumb. Really, Brad. Let's take you to a doctor and get it over with."

It is a funny thing but Brad has never never gotten mad at Tyler.

In fact he vacillates between the two inappropriate, somewhat school-boyish sentiments of awe and fierce affection.

But this time he does get angry. If Tyler is like an upperclassman, Brad is like a sophomore who can take no more bloody solicitousness. Never losing control, knowing that Tyler will not comprehend him now, he bares his teeth in a parody of a schoolboy smile and lets his voice go a little high-pitched, a little testy.

"I'd prefer that you just purchase the Band-Aid, Tyler. There's a good fellow."

Tyler finally looks Brad in the face and screws up his eyes a little.

"I *am* sorry," he says, and his voice is softened by what might be a bona fide remorse. After all, it is Brad who often speaks nastily, ironically, and Tyler who can always be trusted to mean what he says.

Later Brad goes out into the night air, where there is at last a coolness from off the distant ocean, an atmosphere, as well as a crackling Rice-Crispies sound of insects flying into blue electrocution panels. Breathing deeply, he sits cross-legged on top of his giant red backpack and holds both thumbs, patient and nurse, up into the breeze. From where he sits he can see a yellow and black sign with a thick red arrow and the words "A-Okay, Campground of America."

Soon Tyler comes ambling toward him across the asphalt, holding a white paper bag tight to his chest, and Brad realizes, with a mild disapproval, that Tyler has taken time to do some extra shopping in the ministore. Flopping down onto his own backpack, Tyler reaches in the paper bag and ceremoniously places a cardboard box of Band-Aids on the ground.

"Five hundred? When I asked for one?"

"Better to be prepared. Who knows what part of your body you—or I—might decide to injure next?"

"What else did you get?"

"Take a look. A box of donuts. A quart of milk. A good idea. It's smart to eat something after you've lost blood."

"And," says Brad, "I see you went to the trouble of getting me donuts with red jimmies. In honor of the lost red blood cells?"

Tyler considers this comically intended analogy as he might consider a political opinion, and then frowns.

"No, Brad," he replies. "That was the only kind they had."

The women's bathroom is the only spot in the campground with a light bright enough for reading. Before he goes back in Brad makes sure to take the knife off the belt loop and, because there is no one else camping at the A-Okay that night except an old man in a mercury-blue suit and a black baseball cap who seems to be traveling by himself, he ends up stripping off his cut-offs entirely and goes to read wearing only his glasses, his underwear, and a T-shirt. Without thinking about it he goes into the same stall where he had the accident, lifts the lid on the toilet, and is bewildered at first by the reddish black coagulations that float in the bowl of golden urine.

Who's been eating their toast and jam in here? he thinks.

"No, that's wrong," he says out loud, and laughs at his memory lapse. "Someone has been bleeding and pissing and pissing and bleeding at the same time."

Brad sits down and out of boredom picks up a piece of paper that someone has left lying on the floor of the next stall over, but which he can just reach. It is notebook paper, three-hole punched, blue with pinkish lines, and a few lines have been filled with light, hard-to-read penciling. It is clearly a letter that someone has started and not finished, and with a mixture of interest and guilt, Brad squints at the difficult handwriting.

"Dear Beautiful Sarah," it reads. "I'm writing to you from a smelly bathroom stall at an A-Okay camp south of Luxorville. Still on my way to Mexico. I am traveling with a funny guy named Brad."

Brad reads the letter again and again, and thinks, why doesn't Tyler remember that Sarah knows who he is, that they had met that very morning when she came by to sublet the apartment? And he guesses that the reason this letter is lying on the floor is that Tyler didn't like this beginning to his letter and started over on a new page.

And finally he wonders, what does it mean when Tyler says, "funny"?

When Brad emerges from the restroom half an hour later he is exhausted, not from reading his book but from attempting to make sense of the letter, and thinks only of crashing. Tyler, however, is not only still up but deep in conversation with the old man in the blue suit and baseball cap. From a distance it looks like an argument: the old man sits stiffly on the hood of his old-fashioned automobile, his arms folded tight, his legs and waist enclosed in a half-zipped sleeping bag in such a way that his upper body looks squeezed from a tube. Tyler, meanwhile, reclines on one elbow on the pavement below, occasionally waving his free arm in the air to make a point, and then bringing his hand down violently to slap at an insect on his neck.

Oh brother, says Brad to himself. When he gets up close to the two he says it again, not quite to himself.

They look at him.

"Doctor LeBaron," says Tyler, after a pause, "this is my friend Brad, the one I was telling you about. Brad, didn't I tell you I'd find you some medical help? Doctor, take a look at my friend's thumb, please."

The old man smiles, says nothing, makes no move to inspect the bandaged thumb that Brad automatically holds out for him to see. He is clearly over seventy, less than eighty, a little over five feet tall. A trim little beard gives him a polished appearance, despite the cap and the sleeping bag, which Brad can see now is the old-fashioned cotton kind, its lining printed, like wallpaper in a men's club, with vignettes of a hunter leveling his gun at some ducks. When Tyler introduces the man as a doctor, Brad immediately thinks *quack, quack* to himself—though he doesn't know why. What is most surprising to him is the old man's voice. Between sips of root beer from a can that seem to lubricate and enhance them, the syllables are elegant, full of "broadcast quality," yet somehow sour and threatening at the same time.

"You've got quite a friend here in your friend Tyler," says the old man, finally taking hold of Brad's hand, but only to shake it, squeezing the injured thumb painfully, and lifting himself out of his bag an inch or two to peer into Brad's eyes.

"Hey, what's he been telling you?" mutters Brad, looking at the ground. He is thinking about that Jiminy Cricket voice.

"Oh he's been talking my ear off," laughs the old guy, rotating a fingertip in one ear as if to ream out the accumulated lecturing. "But what counts is what I've been telling him, young man. And I've been telling him what I will now tell you. That you'd be smart to be smart enough to listen to what the doctor tells you."

Yes it is Jiminy: avuncular but flat, sentimental but a little smart-assed.

"Doctor LeBaron," says Tyler, pronouncing the name with a certain drama, "has lived in Mexico. And listen to this, Brad. I told him my idea about the job in La Fábrica del Pueblo, and he thinks it sounds splendid. Right Doctor?"

The doctor does not yet let go of Brad's hand, nor relax his frightening stare.

"I believe you suffer greatly from headaches," says LeBaron, frowning, compassionate, taking another sip from his root beer but still holding on to the hand.

"Oh God," says Tyler, "I never told him that. He's diagnosing you, Brad. He's good at what he does."

Brad in fact has had a bad headache all that afternoon—and he realizes now that it really disappeared the moment he cut himself—but he isn't sure if LeBaron is actually evaluating the ills of one day or of a lifetime and so hesitates to answer.

"Come on, Brad," Tyler frowns, wagging his head a little, speaking through his nose. "Didn't you tell me you have a history of migraines?"

Finally Brad pulls his hand away from the doctor's and smiles.

"Doctor," he says, deciding, for once, to ignore Tyler's depressing and patrician tone and to make a joke out of the whole thing, "today I had a headache so bad I could hardly keep from grabbing the wheel away from our driver and forcing the car off the road and into a tree. And look at my thumb. Someone told me that if you let a little blood out, especially blood from the thumb, you can cure a nasty headache. So I think what the heck? And I took out my Swiss army knife—"

"Oh shut up, Brad," snaps Tyler.

And Brad understands for the first time that this is something his roommate cannot stand: conversation that slips a little beyond his control.

But LeBaron isn't laughing at Brad's joke either. He appears to be as put off by, or as uncomprehending of, the irony as Tyler.

"You know what's wrong with you boys?" he finally says, perhaps irritated. "You boys are two boys who need a Reverse-All treatment." The doctor returns to his root beer, and he holds the bottom of the can toward the stars, and guzzles down the last drops like a thirsty child. When he is through he zips up his sleeping bag all the way to his chin and stretches out on the hood of his car in such a way that his head nearly rests on the windshield wipers.

"Do you sleep on the hood of your car?" asks Brad. But the old man appears to be close to dozing off already, and Tyler leads his friend away by the elbow, holding a finger to his lips.

The next morning they walk the half mile back to the highway and try thumbing again, but there are no more than six or seven cars per hour and by noon they are disillusioned, disgusted with the world, morally depleted. At five o'clock, Tyler suddenly hoists his backpack to his shoulder and starts walking back toward the A-Okay. And Brad follows.

That night, however, Brad feels better than ever, filled with a strange feeling that he wouldn't care if they never got a ride, that they could stay in the A-Okay for months and have a good time. One of the things he knows he wants to do while they are there is to rewrite Tyler's letter to Sarah. It is an easy, silly thing to do, and he thinks of it at first as more like filling in a crossword than intruding on his friend's privacy. The bathroom stall is the only place with enough light to work by and there he reads the letter over again:

Dear Beautiful Sarah,
I'm writing to you from a smelly bathroom stall at an A-Okay camp south of Luxorville. Still on my way to Mexico. I am traveling with a funny guy named Brad.

Then Brad, making no great effort to copy his friend's penmanship, writes:

Brad is not funny in that he's strange, but funny in that he's amusing. He tells jokes, makes funny faces, keeps us from killing ourselves when we're hitchhiking, without getting a ride, for eight straight hours. If we don't get a ride tomorrow we'll just have to think about giving up. Going back to school, to the apartment? No, I could never deal with the humiliation. I'll jump off the roof of the A-Okay office, or lie down in the road in front of a semi before giving up.

But the following day is the same story. "What the fuck is wrong with people these days?" screams Tyler after one car pulls over so decisively that he leaps up from the ground and grabs at his backpack, only to discover that the driver has stopped to open his door a crack, dump what looks like a bag of garbage on the ground, and then speed off. "Do they think we're murderers? Do they think we're Lerner and Lowe?"

"That's Leopold and Loeb," offers Brad.

But Tyler is still kicking at clumps of old asphalt, still dancing with rage. "Do they think we're Charlie Fucking Manson?"

"I think," says Brad, prodding with his toe the grocery bag that their tormentor has left behind, "I think they think we are refugees. Come look at this stuff."

It is not a bag of garbage, or at least doesn't seem so to two poor students. Inside are treasures: two shirts, neatly folded as if fresh from the laundromat, one a black and yellow cowboy plaid with steel snaps for buttons, and the other a mechanic's blue workshirt with the name "Buzz" embroidered over the pocket.

That night the campground is a little cooler than before, and for the first time in months Brad feels a little uncomfortable in his cutoffs. They do at least have the extra shirts and these they slip on over the T-shirts they're already wearing. Brad gets the cowboy shirt, Tyler the Buzz shirt. Neither of them bother to button. They are both pleased, but say nothing, because neither feels like talking to the other. Brad goes to sit in his stall, takes out the letter again, and picks up where he left off the night before:

Anyway, I recall now that you met Brad the morning we left. Do you remember what a great guy he is? When I get back we'll all get together. In fact, it's a strange fantasy of mine that you and Brad will make love. You could wear that thin cotton dress, the seaweed-brown one, with the row of twenty or thirty buttons down the front. I name you, in this fantasy, Aphrodite. I picture you lying on top of him while he slowly undoes those buttons, one at a time, until you stop him halfway down, sit up, and pull the dress over your head. Underneath you are wearing no panties, but a black bra, the kind that hooks in the front, and when he unfastens it your breasts tumble out into his face, and he takes one nipple at a time into his mouth while he slowly spreads your legs with his hands and goes on to fuck you and fuck you and— oh yeah—and fuck you.

After this installment he rises to masturbate, staring at himself in the stainless steel mirror above the sink. In the ghostly distortions and scratches of the steel he looks to himself like a long-haired, long-dead wraith, and the movements of his arm and hand look like incantations, or curses.

"What you need, Tyler," the doctor is saying when Brad comes back outside, "is a good session of Reverse-All. Reverse-All is the Key to Everything, the Clue I can give you to a Better Life. Put on your thinking cap, Tyler, and tell me you wouldn't be better off after following my simple suggestion."

Above them five round flat clouds, the color of semen, bear off in parallel lines toward a vanishing point above the mountains of Mexico.

Brad can make no real sense, finally, of the words themselves. He even says the phrase to himself, under his breath: Reverse-All. The only reversal treatment he can imagine needing is the one he and Tyler are already in the middle of, that is to say, their reversal of fortune. It is this: the idea of hitchhiking to La Fábrica del Pueblo, the ambition of securing employment just across the border, the notion, however illusory, of making enough money—even if it is just a hundred dollars!—to reverse themselves forever out of the basin of defeat and absurdity where they have spent forty collective years, and that they concur in regarding as the one and only region where they cannot bear to live another lifetime like the one they have already passed there. It occurs to Brad that Tyler has told the old man so much about them already that LeBaron is talking about all this, even celebrating this, in all his talk of Reverse-All, of reversal.

Or, as seems more likely, more mundane: is Reverse-All merely a type of medical treatment? If so Brad is also interested, because his thumb has begun to throb again as painfully as the first night, as painfully as if a secondary heart is beginning to grow there. He has read how quacks—homeopaths, he thinks they're called—administer such low dosages of medicine that no harmful side effects can result, while at the same time the molecules may bring just the right level of comfort and cure to the affected area. He believes that if he acts more politely the doctor may well give him the necessary molecules.

As he waits and thinks and gets lost in thought, there is a change in the night air then, a jerk or shift toward darkness, as if the lights of some distant city, some unknown and tantalizing metropolis in Mexico, have all been turned out at once. It seems like the end of the evening.

And Brad turns back to say goodnight. But the old man and Tyler and the car are gone. For the first time he notices a thick smell of rain in the air. A second later, before he has time to wonder what has happened, there is a startling blast of a nearby horn, and Brad wheels to see the doctor's car parked at a strange angle on one of the old drive-in ridges. Tyler is leaning out the window of the doctor's car, gesturing frantically.

"Come on, Brad, get in the car. Doctor LeBaron has invited us to visit his house, I mean his clinic. Well, he says they're the same thing."

"Where in tarnation is it?" mutters Brad to himself in a Yosemite Sam voice, coming up with a pretty good impersonation but knowing it would be useless to try to make himself heard over the wildly sputtering engine. He hates, really, to get into the car and thinks wildly for any excuse not to. The A-Okay suddenly seems like home, and he wonders if it might not be possible to stay somehow—to get a job pumping gas, selling doughnuts, raking the gravel into swirling, Zen patterns over the ribs of the terrain.

"Get in, asshole," Tyler leers, and Brad reluctantly grabs his backpack and dives into the back seat. When the engine quiets to a relative purr he is the first to speak.

"Where is it? Where's the house? The clinic?"

"Nearby," Tyler smiles, looking back at Brad and solemnly perching his chin on top of the front seat.

"Then why is he living at the A-Okay?"

But by then the doctor has gunned the engine back to a dreadful, rocketlike roar, the car has begun to lurch cautiously forward, and either Tyler doesn't hear Brad's question or he can't answer it, because he merely nods and turns back to watch how LeBaron expertly guides the car out onto the highway at frightening speed.

After a long time of driving over a flat landscape on a glistening black freeway that seems to Brad like an endless oil spill, the doctor is the first to break the silence, and he does so in an unexpected way: with a song.

"Powered by the Thunderhead, charged by the multiple manifold, paced by the overdrive," he chants in a clean high voice, full of harsh, almost European *r*'s. "And antitheft protection provided by Smith and Wesson," he sings.

Finally Brad sits up straight on the edge of his seat and, putting his lips against the back of Tyler's ear, whispers, "What's he singing?"

"My friend in the back," says Tyler to LeBaron, while Brad sits back and winces, "would like me to ask you about the drift of your lyrics."

"Don't you know that jingle?" smiles the doctor, jaunty and youthful, for a moment, behind the wheel. "It's the song you always have to sing when driving one of these cars. It's the song for this car, don't you see?"

"Doctor LeBaron, I imagine that yours has been a life of self-motivated success," says Tyler.

"Not at all," shoots back the doctor. "I wasted most of my life teaching at a junior college around here. It's only now, Tyler, in retirement, that I consider myself a successful man."

"You taught at the college? At India? Why that's amazing. My friend and I just happen to be students there."

Brad sits silently in the back, staring at the knuckles of LeBaron's right hand. The hand, clutching the steering wheel in the two o'clock position, is bathed in a medicinal green light from the speedometer numbers but looks old to Brad, and skeletal. He doesn't care for the way Tyler is talking to the old man, and he especially doesn't like Tyler giving out information about the two of them.

"I knew you were students at the college," the doctor smiles at Tyler. "I could see that right away. You wouldn't have known me there, because I never worked with boys like you."

"Come to think of it, I think I have seen your name on a plaque or something."

Brad knows that Tyler is lying, and hates it.

"The only plaque they ought to put up for me over there is one that says that I'm the only teacher who ever worked there who learned—for the college's sake, mind you—how to fly an airplane. Can you believe that? Out of hundreds of faculty over the years? You know, I'd like to take both of you fellows flying one day. Ever been up in a private plane?"

"Not me, that's for sure. What about you Brad? Want to try it?"

Brad closes his eyes and pretends to be asleep.

"What I like to do, Tyler, is take students up to see the pictographs. Ever see the pictographs out by the lake? Scratched in the dirt by an ancient tribe, those pictures. My religion—RLDS if you know what that is—tells me that they are put there by descendants of the Israelites. And it's true. From the air you can see that one of them begins to take on the shape of the Ark of the Covenant. Most people don't have any idea that that's true."

"What's amazing to me, Doctor LeBaron," says Tyler, quietly turning to tap on Brad's knees as he speaks, as if trying to get his friend to wake up and participate, "is that people don't want to learn about that sort of thing. If they did, they'd have to rewrite our history books, wouldn't they?"

The old man laughs. "That's right, son. You got that right all the way. You're what they used to call a whippersnapper, aren't you? You know, if I didn't already have somebody, I'd hire you to help me out in my business right away."

They drive on then, in silence except for the animallike humming of the Thunderhead and the nasal sound of rubber tires against newly paved road. Tyler flashes Brad a wan, self-conscious smile, which Brad watches through his half-closed eyes. That is Tyler all the way, he thinks. The kind of guy whose main triumph in life is to appear to synchronize with everybody, to make friends with "representatives," as he has put it himself once, in all seriousness, "from all walks of life."

But more to the point, why can't he, Brad, do the same thing? Why can Tyler, who is so formal and so pedestrian, impress people so much more easily than he, Brad, who is—at least so it seems more and more to himself—relatively clever, relatively interesting? Maybe because he sits around asking himself questions like these?

When Brad looks out the window again he is surprised to find that they have left the highway and are now bumping along a darkened dirt road, far from lights or billboards. A moment later they pull into a driveway marked by a sign that reads, in part, "Casa de Recycled Appliances."

It is difficult to see in the dark, but the roommates, once out of the car, can make out that they have ended up in a kind of shabby but well-lit yard. There are three or four gray buildings, a small mobile home below them at the bottom of a slope, all fringed with weeds and scattered trash. The doctor, sullen and squinting now, wordlessly directs the two travelers toward the door of a tiny, cinder-block building. From the outside it is dark and unappealing, a low-budget version of a mad doctor's laboratory, thinks Brad, with a number of empty propane tanks scattered near the door and a single window covered with black plastic sheeting and duct tape. LeBaron fumbles at the door with his key, whimpering strangely to himself. At last it opens, then there's a screen door to open, and finally he hustles them into a confusing, brightly lit interior.

They are where he seems to want them to be.

LeBaron disappears then, leaving them to throw their backpacks on the floor and wander aimlessly under the whitewash of fluorescent tubes. Brad can't help but worry. Then worry about worrying.

It is a vaguely clinical interior. Along one wall there are four massive, reclining lounge chairs, upholstered in medical green, with little stainless steel tables that swivel off to one side. There is absolutely nothing in it to suggest that it is more sinister than a dentist's office. Brad jeers out loud, Yosemite Sam again, that it is probably a beauty salon for desert rats. The joke falls flat. One entire wall is papered with a life-sized photograph of a green and sun-flecked forest. Against that wall, as if set up for a committee meeting in the woods, is a row of metal folding chairs and a pair of TV trays holding loosely scattered stacks of magazines and Styrofoam plates and tongue depressors. The boys search for a long time for a way to settle in, for a way to become part of the room. Finally Tyler stands with legs apart and thumbs through some of the magazines, while Brad reclines, eyes closed, in one of the green leatherette loungers.

"I've never understood why some doctors put out their medical magazines in their waiting rooms," says Tyler. "Do they imagine patients would want to read them? Just look at these titles. Designed to inspire confidence in the patient? Listen to these: *Modern Thrombosis. Hemodialysis Abstracts. Journal of Trauma.*"

"*Journal of Trauma?*" Brad sits up in his chair. "That's fantastic, Tyler. That sounds like the diary of some kind of existentialist. Or a newspaper that only writes about disasters. Hey, Tyler. It sounds like our day, today, don't you think?"

"If you mean our trip to the doctor, no. I guess I'm a little put out by just sitting around here wondering what's going on, wondering when we're going to get to Mexico. And here we are just a few yards, I think, from the international border. It feels like we've come a thousand miles today and there's still a thousand miles to go."

Now comes a heavy knocking. Shave and a haircut. Brad bolts out of the lounger, expecting to see LeBaron again, expecting to finally allow himself to spit out his gathering anger and tell the doctor something—he isn't sure what—about what he thinks of the whole business. He walks a few steps and flings open the door.

But it is not the doctor. Framed in the screen door is a girl, a teenager, with thin blonde hair and a somewhat masculine face and thick interesting lips that give her the pouty expression of a rock and roller—a Pat Benatar or a David Lee Roth.

"May I help you?" asks Brad, leaning against the doorjamb, aware of the sharp metallic odor of the screen. He thinks it's funny that he says that as if he is the host and the blonde girl is an uninvited guest.

The teenager, not answering, opens the door and walks in, ducking a little under Brad's outstretched arm.

"You guys want the procedure?" she mutters, still without raising her eyes, without, apparently, wanting ever to make eye contact. Brad glances at Tyler with a comically arched, Mr. Spock eyebrow, and then both of them turn to watch as the young woman, suddenly angelic in her long hair but a little rough in her movements, stands near a table and methodically gathers together some glass bottles, some rubber hose, and some syringes. She wears cut-offs just like Brad's.

"Of course we want the procedure," growls Tyler, sprawling back on the green lounger that Brad has just abandoned. "I do get to go first, don't I? Reverse-All? Is that what you're talking about? Sure. I'm ready." And he straightens his feet carefully and crosses his hands just above his crotch, as if preparing for dental hygiene.

The girl smiles and Brad realizes around that point that this is not a girl or a teenager at all, but a woman about their own age, about twenty, whose long hair and thin boyish body give the impression of adolescence.

Brad is worried about the Reverse-All. He thinks he ought to do something to keep Tyler from submitting to whatever it is, but he finds himself trying to dissuade the stranger, instead of what would be wiser, arguing directly with Tyler.

"I don't think you should do anything to him before we talk a little bit first," suggests Brad meekly, though inside he is really feeling something that is perhaps a little like panic. It occurs to him that the main result of the treatment, whatever its purpose, could be to dull the intelligence, and that Tyler's joyless but rational pedagogy is the one thing he cannot afford to lose.

"That's right, Brad. That's right." It is Tyler, lunging to his feet again and coming face to face with the two others, so that they stand in a small knot in the middle of the room, as if at a cocktail party.

"What's your name?"

"Tracy. And," squinting at Tyler's shirt pocket, "yours is Buzz."

"Tracy, I'd like to offer you a little of our marijuana." Tyler fishes for and pulls out a cigarette.

"What's that?"

"Brad, she's never heard of marijuana."

"She's joking, Tyler."

"If LeBaron came in right now he'd shoot all three of us dead," murmurs Tracy, without a trace of either irony or anxiety. "Didn't you wonder why he wears a suit in this weather? He carries a gun like a cop, in a holster under his armpit."

"Are you suggesting we go outside?" asks Tyler, his words muffled by the dainty cigarette he has placed like a toothpick between his lips.

It is exactly three o'clock in the morning when they step out into the night air, and the moon has finally risen: a hard slice of rock above the ragged hills. Standing in a small circle, each with legs spread slightly and planted firmly in the dirt, heads bent forward a little conspiratorially, they busy themselves with the ritual of the smoke, and say nothing. As the cigarette makes its rounds, each one's face is for a moment illumined, at first just faintly by the glowing paper and grass, then brightly as the slow, noisy intake of breath feeds the ember into brilliance. Tyler occasionally makes an enigmatic gesture while his lungs are full. Tracy, while waiting her turn, looks away from the others, staring across the bleak landscape, flipping her hair off her neck every few seconds with a funny roll of the head. Tyler finally breaks the silence.

"Shit, I'm *almost* getting cold."

"Shit, I'm hot," counters Brad.

"You guys should trade shirts," suggests Tracy.

The two guys stare at her for a moment, and then, quietly, uncomfortably peel off their outer shirts and switch, so that Tyler ends up with the steel snaps and Brad the short sleeves.

"Now your name," she says to Brad, "is Buzz."

Then there is more smoking, more silence. Brad sometimes peers nervously at the other two as if he, not Tracy, is the outsider. He almost has to laugh at himself because he finds himself watching for a clue that they accept him, and like him. But when it comes his turn to inhale he forgets all that for a moment and concentrates on getting high, on Sarah, on getting to Mexico, which he knows is very close, perhaps just at the crest of the moonlit hills. Maybe those rocks are Mexican rocks, he thinks. Maybe that moon is in Mexico.

Back inside, Brad sees for the first time a thing he cannot believe is real. What he sees is a paperweight on top of a stack of medical journals. It is a sphinx and when was he recently talking about a sphinx? Oh yeah. Far out. Let's see: in a way it seems to him that he has never not been stoned, that being stoned is what is normal, that this lugubrious, painfully revelatory, half-blind state of mind must always be, because without it there could never be two sphinxes, the one he dreamed of and the one which he is druggily perspicacious enough to discover now: a roughly cut miniature of the Egyptian monument. It is made of alabaster the color of dishwater.

"Look at this, Tyler," he mumbles, but Tyler is already reclining like a duke in one of the green loungers, and Tracy is rushing about, busying herself with tools and tubes, turning on a noisy little apparatus next to the lounger, all as if she and Tyler have come to some private agreement about the procedure while Brad wallowed in his pharaoh's reverie.

When Tracy walks away for a moment and busies herself on the other side of the room, Brad lunges over to sit down in the lounger next to Tyler's. "What are you doing?" he whispers. "What is she going to do to you, Tyler?"

Tyler looks coolly at Brad out of hardened, sphinxlike eyes and speaks with what seems like unusual precision and eloquence. "Don't you know? Come on. Don't you realize what this all represents to us, Brad? We've lucked into something here with Doctor LeBaron and his nurse or daughter or whatever she is. Do I need to spell it out to you? For you?"

Brad swallows, and shrugs.

"Plasma," says Tyler. "We're going to sell our plasma. I guess you missed that part when I was talking to LeBaron on the car, and you were still in the A-Okay bathroom. Listen, Brad, he pays forty dollars per contribution. Well of course contribution's the wrong word; this isn't like the Red Cross. At any rate, that's more than you can get almost anywhere. That's as much as we can make tomorrow cleaning up Mexico's Three Mile Island, or Bhopal, or whatever they have in store for us there. Haven't you ever sold your plasma before?"

"No."

"What about blood? Did you ever give blood?"

"Sure."

"Well then, you've sold your plasma. It's just that they didn't separate it. What's fantastic about plasma is that's all they take; Tracy here will very generously, very thoughtfully give you all your red blood cells, all the important cells, back. See the machine? That's a centrifuge. Isn't it noisy? Your blood goes in, gets spun around. The plasma, which is only this kind of thin yellowish stuff, like piss really, goes down one tube, into their plasma bank, and the red cells and even the white cells are redirected, 'reversed' back into your veins. LeBaron claims it's good for you. He says the blood cells are more potent when they get back into your blood, and you get some kind of supercharged feeling from it. Anyway that's it. They unplug you, you stand up, Tracy hands you your forty dollars, and you walk away knowing that some, you know, sick person in an orphanage or a hospital is going to get better, thanks to you."

All this is spoken in a whisper, rapid and intensely cogent, like a legal argument.

"All right," says Brad, "but I think I've already given enough blood for one day." He holds up his thumb and there, as if to prove his point, it can be seen that the wound has kept bleeding awhile; the thin strips of gauze that peek out over the edges of the plastic are brown and stiff with Brad's blood.

"Okay, then, you just watch me, and then you'll want to do it too," smiles Tyler as Tracy comes close with the equipment.

"Have you ever done this stoned before?" asks Brad. But Tyler has closed his eyes and isn't talking.

"Hey, Tracy," Brad continues. "What about that? We're all pretty high. Will his plasma be contaminated with cannabis residues? Herbaceous tars? Will that poor little guy in the orphanage get a surprise high?"

Tracy grins, doesn't answer, just stretches and inverts Tyler's forearm and positions it on the wide arm of the lounger, then dabs at the skin with an alcohol swab. Next comes the needle, but before it goes in the vein Brad turns away, having noted that it is an especially large and horrible one, with a hole in the tip so large that it looks more like a little sharpened hose than a needle. Then he looks back, because it occurs to him that he would like to see Tyler in pain and stripped of all his seriousness for once. But as Tracy bends over and shoves the point into a prominent vein, Tyler sighs and smiles, as if the needle were not hollow and ready to drink but full of some efficient drug.

Brad goes outside and walks around for a while, too sad to think straight. On one side of the plasma clinic, he pauses to look up at the low ridges and hills, and there he gets a shock: it seems that the slopes not far above him are strung with rows of dim gray houses, hundreds of them, each one square and squat and barely visible in the darkness, with blacked-out windows and leaning walls that suggest a long period of disrepair.

They must be abandoned, is his first thought.

Maybe I could live in one, is his second, and he begins to climb toward them. He is knee-deep in thistles and dusty weeds before he stops, peers again, rubs his eyes, and realizes that they aren't houses but old stoves: the recycled appliances advertised in LeBaron's sign.

He is pretty sure then, as he turns and walks slowly down the hill, back toward the clinic, that he will not go to Mexico. The whole proposition appears just as it should have appeared from the beginning: as an ugliness, a devastation, a turkey. The idea of immigrating backwards is asinine. Mexicans come to the U.S. to work in factories, not vice versa. That's what Reverse-All might as well mean, he concludes. Reverse two countries, reverse their citizens. And if the reversal is complete, he reflects, he would find himself not only working for low wages in some hazardous factory, but maybe even subject to insulting jokes and discriminations. No. With the money he will make selling his plasma, he can catch a bus back home, move in with his parents again, start the new semester at India, and look for something less exotic but less doubtful. Something less fascinating but less dangerous. Something less Mexican.

Brad sighs, puts his hands in his pants pockets, and there finds the roach of the cigarette the three of them have shared before. Tyler has taught him how to use his fingernail to split, lengthwise, the flimsy cardboard of a match, and in this way he makes a pair of rude tweezers, then lights the cradled roach and sucks in the remaining smoke and warmth.

"Hey, any left for me?"

It is Tracy, coming up to him from out of nowhere, smiling, one hand extended for the joint and the other hand pushing one side of her hair behind one ear.

Still holding his breath, even sucking it in another degree, Brad extends the nearly exhausted cigarette, then turns back to view the ovens with a long, floating exhalation.

"You ready for the procedure, Buzz?" asks Tracy, her voice distorted into a falsetto wheeze by the act of holding her breath and speaking at the same time.

"Okee doke," says Brad, starting to hold his breath again before he realizes that he has not taken a second hit.

When they finally make their way back to the clinic Tyler is not in sight, but Brad thinks little of it at the time and simply plops down in the green lounger.

Then it is his turn for the plasma apparatus. Tracy, Brad sees, is good at her job, even when high. She unwraps packages and sets out instruments with the silence and efficiency of a nurse, or a drug addict. Still, Brad cannot help feeling a little afraid of the enormous needle and gum-colored hose that connects the needle to the centrifuge and which will siphon off his blood, then reverse it back to him when it has been robbed of its serum. And, when the needle finally does go in, it is horrible. Worse than cutting his thumb on the Swiss army knife. Worse than the time, in junior high shop class, a bully mysteriously handed him a fat, three-inch screw and then squeezed his hand so hard that when he opened it he found a bloody spiral cut into his palm. He can only watch bitterly, trying hard to think of the forty dollars, as the point of the needle goes deeper, and the pain will not stop, and shockingly, the translucent hose will not fill up with his blood.

"Oh wow," says Tracy. "I was just reading about this in the journal. Your vein's collapsed. That means, like, the walls of your vein aren't really strong enough for this." As she speaks she tugs the needle out, firmly places a cotton ball over the puncture, and expertly fixes a Band-Aid over the ball.

It is all over.

Brad can't believe it. "What about another vein?" he almost shouts, dreading that the answer will be yes.

Tracy just shakes her head. "I'm sorry, Buzz. I don't want to try it. According to what I read, the result might be the same."

"What about . . ." Brad feels utterly degraded now, staring into the depths of the wallpaper forest, where for a moment he thinks he can make out a hunter with his rifle among the trees. "What about my forty dollars?"

"Sorry again. The doc's got the cash and he's pretty hard-assed. And like he'd know by tomorrow if we tried to cheat him. Looks like you're out in the cold. Really. I mean I'm really sorry. Did it hurt really bad?"

"No. Besides, it's my second wound of the week," smirks Brad, holding up his bandaged thumb. "I'm starting to get Spartan about it. Is it the Spartans or the Trojans who didn't feel pain?"

"Spartans. I think. Weren't the Trojans the ones with the Trojan horse? The Trojans were wimps, man."

"So I guess I'll see if Tyler will split his forty dollars with me."

"Oh-oh. Jeez, I don't know how to tell you this. You might be in for another bummer, I guess. You don't know that Tyler already left?"

"What are you talking about?"

"He told me that as soon as he went up to the house and got his forty dollars from the doc, that he'd head out. Said he was going to walk to the border."

Brad stands up groggily and takes a few leaden steps to where he and Tyler had left their backpacks.

It's true. Tyler's pack is gone.

"I can't believe that he'd just take off without telling me."

"Maybe he looked for you. I had to walk around for a while before I found you out back."

"It's still bizarre." Brad sits down on his backpack, telling himself that he is more stunned than he really is. Of course he can't help but recall that a few minutes before he had been wondering how to get away from his traveling companion. "What do you think could be the problem with an asshole like that?"

"Hey. Wait a second. He's your friend, isn't he? I don't think you should call him an asshole."

"Maybe not. Maybe I'm the asshole."

"Anyway, maybe if we run we can still catch him. The road goes down and around the hill. I know a place where we can stand and look down on the road."

A moment later, they are jogging together. Brad realizes Tracy is an athlete, that she moves like some kind of Olympian. Like a Spartan. They dash along a narrow dirt path, laughing because they are not stoned anymore and the air, now pinkish-gray and warm with predawn light, is so fresh in their lungs and the dew-soaked brush on either side of the trail stings their bare legs as they run. Then they stand at the edge of a cliff and look down, as Tracy has promised, on the road they drove the night before. About two hundred yards away the blacktop runs under the interstate and there, just turning on to a frontage road, they can make out Tyler and know it is him from the backpack, now fantastically and memorably red in the clear new light.

"YAAAAH, TYLER!" shouts Tracy, cupping her hands around her mouth.

Brad puts a hand on Tracy's arm as if to stop her, but then is also moved by an urge to scream and so cups his hands to his mouth too and adds his inspiration and passion to Tracy's. Together their voices have the quality of a plea for rescue and the volume of a yodel—so loud, Brad thinks, as to reach the mountains they can glimpse in the hazy distance. But it is not loud enough to reach Tyler or, if it is loud enough, not terrible or melancholy enough to make him turn around.

Then Brad thinks of the letter. What if Tyler has found it somewhere, read his additions, and marched off toward the border in rage and disappointment? The thought makes him pat his shirt pocket, and then he remembers. They switched shirts. Tyler did find the letter.

In the pocket that he has inherited, he does find a folded paper, but of course it is Tyler's new letter to Sarah, the authentic second draft, the real thing. As the paper unfolds a thinly rolled joint slips out, along with a Polaroid of Sarah, nude and photographically brown. She is crouching on some rumpled sheets, her breasts hanging down as small and sharp as a jaguar's. From the way her arms stretch forward out of the frame it is clear that she is holding the camera, taking the photograph herself.

"Look what I found," he says to Tracy, holding up the joint. Tracy has walked off a few steps to investigate an enormous lizard she has found. She glances over her shoulder, grunts some congratulations, and looks back at the lizard.

"It's a chuckwalla, dude," she says. "It's still so cold and slow I bet I could pick it up as it is and carry it home."

"Well," breathes Brad after awhile, not daring to read the letter, "I guess he must be almost in Mexico by now."

"Who?" asks Tracy, straightening up awkwardly in the sunlight.

"Tyler. In Mexico by now. You think?"

"Whoa, whoa. Time out. Where do you think we are? The U.S. of A.?"

"Well, where do *you* think we are?"

Tracy swings her arms up on top of her head in comic disbelief.

"Buzz, you are in Mexico. Wake up. Be here now, like they say. Your pal Tyler, by the look of things, is headed back to the mainland."

"This is Mexico?"

"Duuhh."

"What?"

"Listen, think about it, Brad. Do you really think a guy like Le-Baron could legally draw and sell plasma in the States? I mean, he doesn't even have a license. He's not an M.D., he's a Ph.D.! In speech and broadcasting! We're like two miles over the border here. If you come on the dirt roads, the way you guys did, you miss the border officials, who know what we're doing here of course. Now you tell me if you can guess why they don't shut us down."

Brad sits down on the ground, tired beyond measure. More abruptly, he stands up again, turns around, and looks back toward the clinic and the other buildings. They are invisible, hidden by the high brush, but there on the ridge, where he has seen them before, but closer now, just a few yards above them, are the old white stoves, now utterly stovelike and unmistakable with their chipped enamel and dirty, greasy insets of glass. Brad can see now that not all of them are equally broken and trashed, but that some are either not so old or have even been fixed up a little.

He has a funny idea then, an urge to stay there with Tracy and Doctor LeBaron, to go to work on all those Mexican stoves.

"Are abandoned stoves like abandoned refrigerators?" he asks Tracy. "I mean, do kids sometimes get locked inside them and suffocate?"

Tracy has turned back to her chuckwalla and doesn't answer. Brad goes on. "I think if you leave an old refrigerator outside there's a law that says you have to remove the door. But all those stoves still have their doors on. What if some kids were playing Hansel and Gretel and decided to crawl in? Didn't you ever feel tempted to do that when you were little?"

Tracy doesn't answer. He opens and reads the letter.

Dear Sarah,

I had to throw away the first letter I was writing you. So this one arrives late. I hope I can say what I want to say in this one. We aren't in Mexico yet. We're staying at some campground near the border. Can't get a ride to save our lives. Well, I hope we get a ride soon. I hate Americans. As soon as we get into Mexico I'm sure I'll hate Mexicans. Planning to go really DEEP into Mexico. Please don't sit around waiting for me to come back. I might and I might not. I know I'll want to be away from the United States for months, maybe years. Somehow I don't think Brad will make it. I get the feeling he's going to head back home any day. I guess he'll want the apartment back. Maybe you two will hit it off. Just kidding. When I masturbated this morning, I was looking at the photo you gave me. Sincerely yours. Tyler.

Brad stares at Tracy's hunched shoulders for a while before he walks over, kneels down beside her to look at the large black lizard on the rock, and starts caressing her back, even though her heavy sweatshirt makes this rather awkward.

But at least she doesn't object to his jabs and caresses. She even turns and flashes a big-toothed smile. And why not, thinks Brad. Here in Mexico, the real Mexico, he will be the real Brad. Or better, the real Buzz: stoned, not stoned, in love, making love, all alone, drowning, not drowning, Mexican.

*The Iowa Short
Fiction Award and
John Simmons
Short Fiction Award
Winners*

1994
The Good Doctor,
Susan Onthank Mates
Judge: Joy Williams

1994
Igloo among Palms,
Rod Val Moore
Judge: Joy Williams

1993
Happiness, Ann Harleman
Judge: Francine Prose

1993
Macauley's Thumb, Lex Williford
Judge: Francine Prose

1993
Where Love Leaves Us,
Renée Manfredi
Judge: Francine Prose

1992
My Body to You, Elizabeth Searle
Judge: James Salter

1992
Imaginary Men, Enid Shomer
Judge: James Salter

1991
The Ant Generator,
Elizabeth Harris
Judge: Marilynne Robinson

1991
Traps, Sondra Spatt Olsen
Judge: Marilynne Robinson

1990
A Hole in the Language,
Marly Swick
Judge: Jayne Anne Phillips

1989
Lent: The Slow Fast,
Starkey Flythe, Jr.
Judge: Gail Godwin

1989
Line of Fall, Miles Wilson
Judge: Gail Godwin

1988
The Long White,
Sharon Dilworth
Judge: Robert Stone

1988
The Venus Tree,
Michael Pritchett
Judge: Robert Stone

1987
Fruit of the Month, Abby Frucht
Judge: Alison Lurie

1987
Star Game, Lucia Nevai
Judge: Alison Lurie

1986
Eminent Domain, Dan O'Brien
Judge: Iowa Writers' Workshop

1986
Resurrectionists, Russell Working
Judge: Tobias Wolff

1985
Dancing in the Movies,
Robert Boswell
Judge: Tim O'Brien

1984
Old Wives' Tales, Susan M. Dodd
Judge: Frederick Busch

1983
Heart Failure, Ivy Goodman
Judge: Alice Adams

1982
Shiny Objects, Dianne Benedict
Judge: Raymond Carver

1981
The Phototropic Woman,
Annabel Thomas
Judge: Doris Grumbach

1980
Impossible Appetites,
James Fetler
Judge: Francine du Plessix Gray

1979
Fly Away Home, Mary Hedin
Judge: John Gardner

1978
A Nest of Hooks, Lon Otto
Judge: Stanley Elkin

1977
The Women in the Mirror,
Pat Carr
Judge: Leonard Michaels

1976
The Black Velvet Girl,
C. E. Poverman
Judge: Donald Barthelme

1975
*Harry Belten and the
Mendelssohn Violin Concerto,*
Barry Targan
Judge: George P. Garrett

1974
*After the First Death There Is No
Other,* Natalie L. M. Petesch
Judge: William H. Gass

1973
The Itinerary of Beggars,
H. E. Francis
Judge: John Hawkes

1972
The Burning and Other Stories,
Jack Cady
Judge: Joyce Carol Oates

1971
*Old Morals, Small Continents,
Darker Times,*
Philip F. O'Connor
Judge: George P. Elliott

1970
The Beach Umbrella,
Cyrus Colter
Judges: Vance Bourjaily
and Kurt Vonnegut, Jr.